Princess

A ROYAL PAIN
IN THE CLASS

by
N.J. HUMPHREYS

Marshall Cavendish
Editions

© 2018 Neil Humphreys and Marshall Cavendish International (Asia) Private Limited

Published by Marshall Cavendish Editions
An imprint of Marshall Cavendish International

A member of the
Times Publishing Group

Other Marshall Cavendish Offices:
Marshall Cavendish Corporation. 99 white Plains Road, Tarrytown NY 10591-9001, USA · Marshall Cavendish International (Thailand) Co Ltd. 253 Asoke, 12th Flr, Sukhumvit 21 Road, Klongtoey Nua, wattana, Bangkok 10110, Thailand · Marshall Cavendish (Malaysia) Sdn Bhd, Times Subang, Lot 46, Subang Hi-Tech Industrial Park, Batu Tiga, 40000 Shah Alam, Selangor Darul Ehsan, Malaysia.

Marshall Cavendish is a registered trademark of Times Publishing Limited

National Library Board, Singapore Cataloguing-in-Publication Data

Name(s): Humphreys, Neil.
Title: A royal pain in the class / by N.J. Humphreys.
Other title(s): Princess incognito.
Description: Singapore : Marshall Cavendish Editions, [2018]
Identifier(s): OCN 1050086446 | ISBN 978-981-48-2868-0 (paperback)
Subject(s): LCSH: Princesses--Juvenile fiction.
Classification: DDC 823.92--dc23

Printed in Singapore

Cover art and all illustrations by Cheng Puay Koon

For A.R.
Thanks for introducing me
to the secret world of Mulakating.

AN INTRODUCTION TO ME

My name is Sabrina Valence and I'm a princess. That's right. I'm a proper, living and breathing princess. I'm not an animated princess, or a soppy movie princess or a birthday princess at one of those lame parties where all the girls wear frilly dresses and pretend to be princesses. I am the real thing.

I am Princess Sabrina of Mulakating, daughter of King Halbutt Valence and Queen Beverly Sisley. Well, that was my mother's surname before she got married. Secretly, she was psyched to marry my Dad and not just because he was the king. She didn't want to be called Sisley anymore. When she was at school, the other girls called her Beverly Sissy from the House of Sissies. She hated that. She much prefers being Queen Beverly from the House of Valence.

That's the other strange thing. We don't really think of ourselves as the Valence family. Our family is called the House of Valence, which is totally stupid when you think about it because we're not a house. We don't even live in a house. We live in a palace. Or at least I used to live in a palace.

But I don't want to talk about that yet. I know I'll get that knotted feeling in the stomach, rather like the time Uncle Ernie was teaching me a spinning hook kick in taekwondo and I landed on my belly.

When I think of the Palace, my eyes sting. My mother says a royal princess shouldn't have stinging eyes in public. We always say "stinging eyes" and then we'd giggle together. We never mention the C-word.

Princesses do not cry.

But they do, you know. They really do, especially when they are told to leave the Palace, especially when they are sent away from their family in the middle of the night, especially when they are alone in a strange place with weird people.

Hang on. I'm losing my train of thought.

My tutor used to always go on about my "train of thought". She was a bit mad like that. She said my thoughts were like too many trains travelling in too many different directions at the same time. I had to drive one train at a time and keep it on one track.

See. I told you. She was nuts.

But the funny thing is, I miss her now. Her name was Miss Cruickshanks, but I always called her Miss Quick-Pants because I'd run to the toilet whenever she arrived. We studied for hours in Daddy's enormous office and I went to the toilet at least ten times every class just to get away from her.

But I miss the old battle-axe now. I miss them all.

Mostly, I miss being able to tell the truth.

Even this homework is a lie and a total waste of my time. Our teacher told us to write about our family and illustrate a family tree. I know she meant draw a family tree, but she said illustrate instead. She's one of those teachers who throws in big words to show off her intelligence.

The homework must be handed in soon. We've all got to take turns to stand in front of the whiteboard and do class presentations. The title is "My Family And Me". It's not exactly original, is it? Why do teachers always tell us to write about ourselves and our families? It's so predictable.

So I'm basically wasting my time. But I don't care. I'm writing my story anyway, my actual story, the real story. On American TV shows, they call this therapy. Well, this is my therapy. I'm going to write the real story of Princess Sabrina of Mulakating, just for me, just to make me feel better and then I'll lock it away in my bedroom drawer. No one will ever read it, not even my Uncle Ernie. When I'm done, I'll scribble down some fake stuff about living with a mad uncle in a new town and going to a terrible school with a wussy teacher who tells me to write a load of old rubbish about my family and me.

That writing will be for my teacher. This writing is for me. This is the real story about a real princess, a princess in disguise, a princess in hiding, a secret princess who just wants to go home, but can't.

This is my true story about living a big, fat lie.

CHAPTER ONE

Daddy called me into the dining room so I knew I'd done something wrong. I never really liked the dining room. It was big and cold and my voice echoed. Other families got their dining rooms from IKEA. Ours looked like a really boring museum. The ceiling was so high that I had to pull my head back to look at all the paintings.

When I saw Mummy sitting beside Daddy, I was absolutely positive that I was in *big* trouble. I think Mummy had stinging eyes. It was hard to tell because they were both sitting at the end of our long dining table. I had never counted the chairs, but I know Daddy's banquets hosted hundreds of very important people. They were really boring people, too.

I walked past the family portraits that hung on the dining room walls. There were so many of them, all refusing to smile, probably because they were stuck in those golden frames. Normal kids kept photos of their relatives on their phones, but my family had to be oil paintings in our dusty dining room.

Mummy *did* have stinging eyes. When I sat down, she was wiping her cheeks with a handkerchief. I had bought her that hankie for her birthday. Actually, Uncle Ernie bought it but I had picked the style and colour.

"All right. What have I done this time?" I asked.

Daddy and Mummy looked at each other and I started to

get really scared. Daddy had stinging eyes, too. Kings *never* have stinging eyes. It's a rule. Kings don't cry. Maybe he had a cold. Yes, that was it. Winter was on its way and the Palace was always freezing, even in the summer.

"You haven't done anything, dear," Daddy mumbled, clearing his throat. He really had a bad cold.

He always called me "dear", too. I found it a bit embarrassing, to be honest. Who wants to sound like a dopey animal with antlers sticking out of its head? The only good thing was the way my father smiled whenever he called me that.

No one ever smiles at me like my father does.

But this smile was a sad smile. His voice was breaking and his eyes were clearly watering. He needed to see a doctor.

"Are you feeling all right, Daddy?" I asked, but I wasn't sure if I wanted him to answer. Not truthfully anyway.

Uncle Ernie always said that a little white lie could sometimes protect a bigger truth. Uncle Ernie really did talk a lot of rubbish. But I wanted to believe him now.

I wanted to hear little white lies from my parents. I wanted them to tell me that everything was going to be all right. But a stupid knot in my stomach was already telling me something else.

"I'm fine," my father replied.

But he wasn't a good actor, not like my mother. She had loved drama at school and once played Cleopatra in the play *Antony and Cleopatra*. I later found out that Cleopatra was the ruler of ancient Egypt. She was practically a queen, just like my mother.

But her acting was really letting her down now. She was trying to look happy, but she wouldn't win an Oscar for this lousy performance. I thought she was almost going to, you know, do that thing that kings and queens cannot do.

Both of them had trouble speaking. They just stared at me with their mouths open. They looked like goldfish trying to burp.

"Is it about the toothpaste?" I asked.

Mummy shook her head.

"It is, isn't it? I know I keep forgetting to put the cap back on, but I will. And the spitting thing, I know you keep telling me, Daddy. When I spit out the toothpaste, I'll wash it all down the plughole. I promise. Can I go now?"

Daddy leaned forward. "Listen Sabrina, in your history lessons, has Miss Cruickshanks ever talked about the politics of our country?"

"Er, yes, I think so, but it's *so* boring," I said honestly. "Whenever Miss Quick-Pants, sorry, Cruickshanks, starts talking about old wars and our great-great-great-great-great grandparents, I usually say I need to pee."

"Oh dear."

"No, it's fine, Daddy. I don't really need to pee. I just tell her that when she starts waffling on. In fact, there was one time, when she started going on about Greek gods, I told her I needed to do, you know, something bigger and she went all red, so I managed to sneak off for at least ten minutes. And then ..."

"Sabrina, please. I need you to listen. We are a constitutional monarchy. Do you know what that means?"

"Er, is that something to do with diarrhoea?"

"What?" Daddy bellowed. His cheeks turned redder than a ripe tomato. "Why do you keep referring to diarrhoea and stuff?"

"Well, whenever Uncle Ernie has a bellyache and rushes to the toilet, he says he has a bad constitution."

Daddy roared with laughter. Even Mummy giggled.

Daddy was still chuckling when he continued his explanation.

"No, a constitutional monarchy is a country that has a royal family, like us, but most of the power is with the politicians in government," he said.

"So it's definitely not about diarrhoea then?"

"No, Sabrina. This is about power and control and who has it in our country. The Royal Family doesn't control the country anymore. We serve our people in different ways."

"Like when we cut ribbons with scissors and wave from the car window?"

Mummy's eyes started to fill with water. "Oh, you really are a clever girl."

"Anyway, as we don't have any real power to make decisions about our country, some people are wondering if we are still needed," Daddy continued.

"Of course we are needed," I replied. "We are the Royal Family. The people need us to wave at them. "

"Not everyone agrees and the bad news is, they are starting to argue about it. These arguments may go on for some time, so ..."

Daddy stopped talking. He grabbed Mummy's hand and held on tightly. They both had stinging eyes now. So did I. I wasn't even sure why.

"So? So what, Daddy?"

Daddy rubbed his eyes and turned to Mummy. "I can't ... I can't do it, Beverly."

Mummy reached for my hand. "Sabrina, we love you more than anything else in the world, you know that, right?"

"Yes, I know that. But why do I feel scared?"

"You don't need to feel scared. We're going to make sure you'll never have a reason to be scared, because we love you. And because we want you to be safe, at all times, we want you to ..."

"We want you to live with the Earl of Parslowe for a while," Daddy interjected.

I was flabbergasted. "The Earl of Parslowe? Really?"

"Yes, Sabrina."

"Wow. That's amazing ... Who is the Earl of Parslowe?"

Daddy grinned through his tears. "Uncle Ernie," he said. "The Earl of Parslowe is your Uncle Ernie."

"Uncle Ernie? But he lives with us at the Palace."

Daddy shook his head slowly. "No, we've asked him to travel overseas for a while."

"Why?"

"To look after you."

"But why do you want me to leave, Daddy?"

"I don't want you to leave," he croaked. "But I need to save your life."

CHAPTER TWO

And that was it. A day later, I was on a plane. And it was a regular plane, too. There were queues to get on board. There were queues to sit down. There were even queues for the toilet. And the smell of the toilet, well, it was like diving into horse manure. Nobody else seemed to mind, but I thought my nose was going to fall off.

I had never been squeezed into a plane with so many strangers. In fact, the only person I knew on the entire plane was Uncle Ernie and he's bonkers.

Well, he's not bonkers. He's just, yeah all right, he's bonkers. He's not even my Uncle Ernie. His full title is The Earl of Parslowe. Apparently, he comes from a long line of Parslowes.

I think he comes from a long line of parsnips.

I'm not even sure what he does. Most normal people have a job. Miss Quick-Pants was annoying and made my brain melt, but she was a teacher. I knew that. It was clear and simple. But Uncle Ernie isn't a teacher, a doctor, a lawyer, a chef or a bus driver. He's an Uncle Ernie. His job is just to be there, all the time.

I have seen photos of me as a baby with my mother, my father and Uncle Ernie. He's mostly only partially in shot, but he's always there, in the background and mostly blurred. Everything he does is blurred. He's a bit dopey, to be honest.

Once the plane took off, he told me all about my new life and identity.

"You can keep your first name," he said. "You can still be called Sabrina."

"Oh thanks," I grunted. "I'm *so* grateful."

My heart was still thumping against my ribcage after saying goodbye to my parents. I was in no mood for Uncle Ernie's gobbledygook.

"Take this seriously, Sabrina, this is important," he whispered, looking around the plane.

"What are you looking for? Spies? Undercover killers who want to poison my apple juice? Maybe they've poisoned the toilets. That's why they smell like a donkey's backside."

"Be quiet. This is serious. You can still be Sabrina. You're young. We're a tiny state and you've never really been in the international media before. So you're not a well-known royal. But just to be on the safe side, you'll be called Sabrina Parslowe."

"No way, no chance, not happening."

"Hey, what's wrong with Parslowe?"

"It sounds like a parsnip. I don't like parsnips."

"You haven't got to eat my name, Sabrina, you've just got to use it."

"My name is Valence."

"Well now, it's parsnip ... Parslowe! Your name is Parslowe, not parsnip and definitely not Valence."

"No. I'm from the House of Valence. My name is Sabrina Valence."

"Yes and Valence is also the name of a royal family that is currently having problems with the Government."

I leaned towards Uncle Ernie. "Well, that's not my fault."

He leaned towards me. "And it's not my fault either."

"So why are you giving me a rubbish surname?"

"Why is my surname rubbish?"

I leaned even closer. "Because it sounds like a parsnip."

He leaned even closer. "Yeah, well, you look like a parsnip!"

Our noses were almost touching. Other travellers were watching us. We started giggling and sat back in our seats.

"Ah, it's ridiculous, Sabrina. I agree. No one wanted any of this, least of all me."

That comment got me angry again.

"What's wrong with your life?" I snapped. "I've lost my parents, my home and my country. What have you lost?"

"I've lost my best friends, my home and my country and I've also got to babysit a snotty-nosed brat like you."

"I haven't got a snotty nose."

"Yes, you have. Look in a mirror."

I grabbed a tiny mirror from my rucksack under the seat.

"Where's the snot? There's no snot on my face."

Uncle Ernie grinned. "You're so easy. Now, are you ready to listen or not?"

"Yeah, all right. But only if you get me a snack from the servant."

"They're not called servants. They're called air stewards. And you are called Sabrina Parslowe. I am Ernie Parslowe, a handyman living happily in the suburbs."

"What are suburbs?"

"A place where families live happily together, have barbeques and play golf. Don't interrupt me."

"Sorry."

"You are staying with me because your parents have been posted overseas with their jobs and they wanted you to stay at home."

"But I'm not at home."

"This is your home for the time being. You're just moving to a small town from an even smaller town to live with your jolly, grey-haired, handsome uncle."

"Who's that?"

"Me!"

"Your hair isn't grey."

"Thank you very much."

"It's white."

"Very funny, now listen carefully. If any nosey parker at school asks about your parents, tell them it's a sensitive subject and you don't want to talk about it. If there are problems with the teachers, you refer them to me. As far as anyone is concerned, you are Sabrina Parslowe from out of town, staying with your favourite Uncle Ernie so you can finish your school education. Got it?"

"Got it."

I watched the other travellers on the plane fiddle with their phones. Uncle Ernie didn't know what he was talking about. He didn't know YouTube or Instagram or Snapchat or WhatsApp. He didn't even own a mobile phone at the Palace.

All his communication was in whispers and even then, he covered his hand most of the time.

Our crazy secret mission would be messed up in a week. If I started school on Monday, the whole world would know who I really was by Tuesday.

I like Uncle Ernie. I might even, you know, the other L-word. Of course, I'd never tell him that, not to his face. He's always been there for me, since I was a baby. He was probably my best friend. But Uncle Ernie was starting to get old. He was getting those thick white hairs up his nose. He repeated himself. He fell asleep in his armchair. He listened to old music. He didn't know about modern stuff for young people.

I felt sorry for him. He thought we still lived in the olden days and I'd be able to change my name and disappear. But his idea was never going to work.

"Uncle Ernie, can you see what everyone is looking at?" I asked.

"Yeah, their mobile thingies."

Uncle Ernie turned his back on me. I tapped his shoulder.

"Uncle Ernie, do you know what they can do on their mobile thingies?"

"Yeah, make calls. Go to sleep."

I kept tapping his shoulder. "But Uncle Ernie, Uncle Ernie, Uncle Ernie ..."

"What?"

"They can do everything on their phones. They can search for anything. The kids at school could Google our country's history and find a million photos of our family."

Uncle Ernie sat bolt upright, like Dracula rising from his coffin. His hair was a right mess. "You mean to say that if an irritating busybody in your new school searches for 'Princess' and 'Sabrina', they might find you on the Internet?"

"Yes!" I cried.

"Oh no," he moaned.

Uncle Ernie grabbed his pillow and snuggled up in his seat. "Just as well I hacked into the Internet, deleted every photograph of you and your family and every mention of you since you were born. I also created a search engine algorithm that will ensure that whenever someone types in 'Sabrina Parslowe', they will immediately be directed to your fake Instagram account. That account has already got photo-shopped pictures of you playing in the small town that you're supposed to have come from, playing in the garden, playing with the neighbour's dog, you know, really cutesy stuff. There's a fake Sabrina Parslowe account on Snapchat, too, with lots of weird photos of you with fancy filters. I thought about doing Facebook, but let's face it, kids don't really use Facebook. Oh, and if anyone searches for either 'Sabrina Parslowe' or 'Sabrina Valence' more than three times, I will immediately be notified, via a secure and private online address. And then, I will track down the person and have him shot."

I didn't know what to say and was speechless for a full two minutes.

"Will you really do that?" I whispered finally.

"No, Sabrina, I'm not going to have anyone shot."

"I knew it! You made all that stuff up, right?"

"Only the bit about being shot. Everything else is true."

"Wow. I mean ... wow. I didn't really think you'd have anyone shot."

Uncle Ernie smiled at me. "Of course not. I'd feed them to the pigs."

"What? Are you serious? You're kidding, right, Uncle Ernie?"

"Goodnight, Sabrina."

"Goodnight."

I turned off my reading light. Darkness never bothered me at the Palace. But I didn't like being surrounded in the dark by lots of people I didn't know on the plane.

"Are you asleep, Uncle Ernie?" I whispered.

"Yes."

"No, you're not. Can I ask a question?"

"No."

"When you lived at the Palace, were you really a handyman?"

"Absolutely. Now go to sleep."

The plane cabin was really gloomy, but I'm pretty sure Uncle Ernie winked at me.

I was terrified of leaving my parents and moving to a new town and school, but at least Uncle Ernie would be there to make things better.

CHAPTER THREE

Uncle Ernie had made things much, much worse. I hated my new town and I particularly hated my new home. How could he bring me to such a freaky place? I expected the house to be small, but it was attached to lots of other houses. Uncle Ernie said it was called a terraced house. I called it a terrible house. There was only one bathroom. One bathroom! I had to share a toilet with Uncle Ernie and he ate far too much curry.

I know I'm lucky to live in the Palace and that's not normal for most people. I'm not dumb like some of the royals I've met from other countries. Prince Singleton can't even tie his own shoelaces and he's fifteen. I'm nothing like that.

But I was still confused about my new home.

Poorer people said we lived on a housing estate. Richer people said we lived in a suburb. I couldn't tell the difference. Every house looked the same to me. There were hardly any gardens for a start. Everyone wanted to park their cars next to their living room windows. It was weird.

And people did stuff themselves, too. They painted their own bedrooms and did their own gardening. When I first arrived, I remember standing at my front door and nothing happened.

"What are you doing?" Uncle Ernie snapped.

He was red-faced and sweating buckets because he was carrying an armchair.

"I'm waiting," I replied regally.

"Waiting for what?"

"Waiting for you to open the door for me."

"No one's going to open the *fabulous* door for you, Sabrina. You're going to open this *fabulous* door and every other *fabulous* door by yourself from now on. So open the door now before I drop this *fabulous* armchair onto your royal toes."

He didn't actually say *fabulous*. He used other words about the door, words he was never allowed to say in the Palace. Royals are not permitted to use such language in public places.

When we unpacked, Uncle Ernie set out the rules for our new home.

"Doors will no longer be opened for you," he said, as he plonked the armchair in our living room. His forehead was leaking.

"In fact, you will open doors for people like me."

"People who are sweating?"

"No!"

"People carrying armchairs?"

"No! Old people! People that are older than you, or people with prams, buggies and wheelchairs."

"Ok, got it. I open doors for all those people. That's easy."

"And you have to talk to people now."

He was a bit of a fruitcake, my Uncle Ernie.

"I know I'll have to talk to people. I've been talking to people my whole life."

Uncle Ernie shook his head. Big globs of sweat flew across the living room.

"No, Sabrina, you've *listened* to people. The royals are trained to *listen* to people. You're trained *not* to speak to people. That way, you can't say anything wrong."

"Oh, like when Daddy shakes hands and does loads of nodding?"

"Exactly. That's called royal etiquette and you were trained in royal etiquette. But that all goes out of the window now, ok? When people talk to you at school, you talk back and pretend you're interested."

Old Uncle Ernie really could get his knickers in a twist at times. How hard could it be to talk to normal people? I spoke to normal people every day at the Palace. I spoke to the gardeners, the cooks, the maids, the dressmakers, everybody. And I must have been a fantastically interesting speaker because they always listened to every word I said. They never interrupted me. They laughed at all my jokes. Sometimes, they even thanked me for talking to them.

"But the other students at school will still bow and curtsey for me, right?" I wondered.

I thought Uncle Ernie was going to burst a blood vessel. A little purple vein above his eye started throbbing. It was gross.

"No, no, no, no, Sabrina, no one is going to bow or curtsey." His voice rose with every word. "You are Sabrina Parslowe living in a small town, in a small house. No one is going to bow or curtsey for you here."

"Pranked ya!" I cried.

I was pretty pleased with that one. Uncle Ernie sighed. He wiped the sweat off his forehead and ran his hand through his hair. He now had a white, spiky Mohawk. I didn't say anything though. His purple vein was still throbbing and my tummy was rumbling. All this pranking was making me hungry.

"What's for lunch?" I asked.

"Sandwiches."

"That's boring. Why sandwiches?"

"A sandwich is the only thing I will trust you to make."

"Why have I got to do it?"

"Because I'm busy and you're hungry."

I was quite excited about making lunch for the first time. I'd seen those TV programmes where the chefs keep swearing at the contestants until they cry. I could do that. I think I'd be an excellent chef.

"Yes, I can totally make a sandwich," I said. "I'm going to make cheese and cucumber. So I need bread and butter, right?"

"That's right."

"And the butter goes only on one side of the bread?"

"Yes, Sabrina."

"That's the side with the sliced cheese and the sliced cucumber."

"Yes, Sabrina."

I went to the fridge and remembered what Uncle Ernie had said. I didn't wait for someone to open the fridge door. I even found the cheese and cucumber, but something had gone terribly wrong.

"Uncle Ernie, you'd better come quickly. I'm having a crisis."

Uncle Ernie dropped the armchair, tripped over one of my suitcases and performed a brilliant forward roll across the hard, wooden floor. He jumped to his feet and must have had a dizzy head because he staggered sideways and whacked his shoulder on the kitchen door frame.

He screamed in pain. "Argh! ... Yes, Sabrina, what is it? What's the crisis?"

"It's terrible, Uncle Ernie. The cheese and cucumber are *not* sliced!"

Uncle Ernie gritted his teeth. He was just as frustrated as I was. I could tell.

"Yeah, I know. You can't believe it, right? " I said. "Maybe the cheese and cucumber aren't sliced in this country."

"THEY AREN'T SLICED IN ANY COUNTRY!"

Uncle Ernie was starting to worry me. He was shouting a lot in the suburbs. Maybe the air was different here. Something was affecting his hearing. Maybe a doctor should check his ears. He was definitely going senile.

"Of course, they are sliced, Uncle Ernie. You must be forgetting because you're getting old. Back in the Palace, the cheese and cucumber on my plate was always sliced."

Uncle Ernie took a really deep breath. He was probably trying to blow out his blocked ears.

"No, Sabrina, the cheese and cucumber was sliced in the Palace because ... you're a princess ... so other people ... you know what? Never mind, I'll make your *fabulous* cheese and cucumber sandwiches."

No, he didn't really say *fabulous*. But I need to be careful. I know this story is private and will be locked away in the drawer beside my bed, but I'm still a princess. One day, I must return to the Palace and I cannot be found with a story that contains inappropriate language.

But as I continue to tell my true story, it's going to get harder to write about Uncle Ernie. He used lots of *fabulous* words when he was slicing the cucumber, especially when the knife slipped and he cut the top of his finger.

"When do you start school again?" he roared, as blood dribbled down his hand.

"On Monday."

"I wish they did Sunday classes!"

Yep, he was totally going senile.

CHAPTER FOUR

The school uniform was green and disgusting. I saw my blazer in that tiny mirror on the car door. I looked like a stick insect with long brown hair. I had woken up early to get my hair right, but there wasn't a hairdo on this planet that could've made my vomit-coloured blazer look any more attractive.

Uncle Ernie's filthy white van made me feel even worse. When he turned the key, the engine farted. All the way to school, the van shook and jolted and farted. In fact, the van reminded me of the puppies we had around the Palace when I was little. They always farted, too.

"I know we can't drive a limo, but did you have to get the noisiest, fartiest van in the universe?" I asked.

"I told you. We're incognito."

"No. We're in a van."

"Incognito means we're in disguise. We're hiding. We can't draw attention to ourselves."

And at that exact moment, the engine did its longest and loudest fart yet, just as we pulled up outside the school. Uncle Ernie thought the engine had exploded. I thought I was going to die of embarrassment.

Smoke poured through the front of the car bonnet. Other children pointed at our rust bucket and giggled. They were all from my new school, too. They were all wearing the same snotty-green blazers.

Uncle Ernie stood over the smoke and waved his arms around like a flapping pelican. The other children laughed at him. I tried to swallow the scratching at the back of my throat. I couldn't have stinging eyes, not on my first day.

"Oh, hello, you must be the new girl."

I spun around in shock. The quiet voice belonged to a boy, and a small boy at that. He was shorter than I was and I wasn't particularly tall.

He also wore glasses. They obviously bothered him because he kept touching the frames. His eyes darted around in all different directions, like a couple of marbles on a floor. He seemed shy and I wasn't sure why. He wasn't ugly. But he wasn't handsome either. Don't get the wrong idea. No boys are handsome. Boys and men can never, ever be handsome, except for my father, of course. But I'm not going to think about him now or I'll get watery eyes.

"Are you the new girl?" the tiny boy asked again.

I realised I had been staring at his funny, zigzagging, brown eyes for far too long. His eyes matched his hairstyle. That was all over the place, too.

"Oh, hello," I said, in my polished princess voice. "And who are you? What do you do? Why have you come to visit me today?"

Uncle Ernie coughed loudly. Through the engine smoke, I saw him shake his head.

Oh no! What an idiot! I'd almost failed my first test! This

boy with the wandering eyes and the windy hair wasn't a royal subject. He was just like me, another student in a horrid green blazer.

"Sorry, I'm a bit jet-lagged from the long flight in the plane ... VAN! I mean, white van, ha ha! Yes, we had a long flight ... DRIVE! I mean, drive ... Yes, we've had a long drive in the white van and you're a subject ... STUDENT! You're a student, like me. Yes, we're both normal, average students. Isn't that funny? Ha ha! And I'm Sabrina of the House of Val ... Val ... FAR AWAY! I mean, my house is far away, well, quite far away. Actually, it's not that far away at all. I don't really know what I'm talking about. Ha ha!"

The tiny boy looked confused. "Er, you're pointing at the school toilets."

"Am I? Yes, I live in the school toilets! Ha ha! No, it's the jet lag! It was such a long journey in the white van from, you know, our small town to your small town ... No, what I mean is, I'm not saying your town is small. It's, like, the perfect size. It's not too big. It's not too small. It's just right! It's like Goldilocks' porridge, ha ha! In fact, all towns in this country should be this size! It's the perfect size! Are all the towns in this country the same size as this town?"

The munchkin just stared at me. At least, he was actually making eye contact this time, which was something. Uncle Ernie held his head in his hands.

"I'm not really sure how big the other towns are," the mini-boy said cautiously.

"Oh, really? Wow. Maybe you should look it up, because this small town is epic."

I realised I was talking too fast.

"Ok. Thank you. So you did say your name was Sabrina?"

"Yes! Yes, my name is Sabrina Parslowe," I said, grinning at Uncle Ernie. "That's absolutely correct. My name is Sabrina Parslowe. That's right. Sabrina Parslowe. It's definitely not Sabrina *Valence*."

I winked at Uncle Ernie. Uncle Ernie looked like he was going to cry.

"Maybe you should go into school now," he mumbled.

"Yes, that's a good idea. I'm supposed to take you to class," the miniature boy chimed in, far too cheerily. "I'm Charles, by the way, but everyone calls me Charlie."

"Thanks, Charlie, that'll be great, won't it, Sabrina? Off you go."

Uncle Ernie shooed me away from the white van like I was a pigeon on his lawn. He put his arm around my shoulder and whispered in my ear.

"Think more. Talk less."

Uncle Ernie was probably right. He usually was, which was annoying.

Still, I tried to follow his smart plan, but something got in the way. Something dark, greasy-haired and horrible.

CHAPTER FIVE

Teachers should not be teachers if they have funny names. That should definitely be a law. No smart adult can be given permission to be a teacher unless he or she has a sensible name. The test would be easy. Each person would stand in front of a class and write their name on the whiteboard. If the children giggle, he or she can't be a teacher. That's it.

And then, as a super safety test, they should also say their name loudly to the class because some names have different pronunciations. They might not seem funny written on a whiteboard, but they can be hilarious out loud. For instance, my old teacher at the palace was Miss Cruickshanks. It doesn't look particularly funny. But the first time she told me her name, I seriously thought I was going to pee myself. She sounded like "Quick-Pants". Even now, I still think of her as Miss Quick-Pants.

But even Miss Quick-Pants doesn't have a name as bad as Miss Shufflebottom.

Shufflebottom! Honestly. That's her real name!

You can say it out loud. Shufflebottom! You can write it on the whiteboard in enormous capital letters. SHUFFLEBOTTOM! You can whisper it with friends or scribble it across a toilet wall. *Shufflebottom.* It's still an epic name.

My teacher's name is Miss Shufflebottom.

In fact, Miss Shufflebottom was the teacher who gave me this homework. She told me to write about my life and my family. She's the reason why there has to be a proper, professional Teacher Name Test.

But her daft name did at least cheer me up. That tiny kid, Charles, didn't stop talking all the way to the classroom. He kept asking if I'd done after-school maths or chess classes at my last school. I had actually done archery, gymnastics and taekwondo with Uncle Ernie at the Palace, but I couldn't tell him that, could I? So I came up with one of my little white lies and mumbled something about cookery and piano. I don't really like either. I'm not a girl from the 1950s. Cooking is boring and who wants to sit in front of a piano playing *Three Blind Mice*? Not me, but I'm not allowed to tell the truth.

And then, I arrived in class and everyone was wearing those putrid blazers. We looked like twenty green bottles hanging on the wall. I thought I was going to throw up my breakfast. Thankfully, my new teacher saved the day.

"Welcome to the class, Sabrina," she said, in a semi-posh voice. "My name is Miss Shufflebottom."

I felt like a balloon. I thought I was going to burst.

"Is everything all right, Sabrina?" Miss Bottom-Shuffler asked.

"Yep," I squeaked.

I opened my mouth no more than half a centimetre. I couldn't risk the laughter escaping through a crack in my lips.

"Yes, what?" she continued.

"Yes, Miss," I hissed. My face and belly were close to exploding.

"Yes, Miss what?"

"Yes ... Miss ... Snuffle ... I mean ... Shuffle ..."

"Yes?"

"Shufflebottom!"

I roared with laughter. I laughed until my jaw ached. I laughed so hard that I made everyone else laugh, everyone except Miss Shufflebottom and a girl who sat alone at the back of the class.

She didn't smile.

She just folded her arms and glared at me.

She had dark, greasy, long hair that looked knotted and in need of a good brushing. Her green blazer had faded, like dried grass in the sun. And she chewed gum in class! I couldn't believe it. Uncle Ernie had already flicked through the school manual, which had made it very clear that gum was not to be chewed in school.

But this girl didn't even care.

In fact, she pulled the gum from her mouth and wrapped it around her finger. Then she spun her finger really quickly and the gum unwrapped itself. She shaped it into a squidgy ball until it looked like the world's tiniest brain, and threw it into the air. She caught it between her teeth and carried on chewing. Everyone heard her teeth grinding.

"Agatha," Miss Shufflebottom said softly. "Not today, eh?"

Everyone turned to face Agatha, the gum-chewing rebel. She didn't seem bothered. She didn't even blush. She just

blew a huge gum bubble instead. The pop echoed around the classroom.

"I think we'll have a quiet chat after class, Agatha," Miss Shufflebottom said. "In the meantime, Sabrina, you seem to have stopped giggling now. Maybe you could join me at the front of the class and tell us a bit about yourself."

I knew what that Miss Silly-Name was doing, all right. It was much easier to embarrass the shy, giggly new girl than deal with the scary, gum-twirling bubble blower at the back.

But I wasn't scared. I was a princess. And this time I had my story straight.

CHAPTER SIX

The thought of speaking in front of the whole class didn't bother me. I had been trained at the Palace to speak in public and in different languages, too. English and French were the easiest, with some Spanish and a tiny bit of Mandarin.

So I stood beside Miss Shufflebottom and tried not to think about her fantastic surname. Luckily for her, she was rather skinny and petite and didn't have much of a bottom to shuffle.

"Hello everyone," I said cheerily. "My name is Sabrina Parslowe and I am eleven years old. I'm almost twelve and we were actually arranging a big party back at the Pala ... I mean, the place ... where I now live. I have just moved to this town with my Uncle Ernie. My parents were posted overseas and—"

"Posted? What are your parents, letters?"

It was the girl with gum. She laughed loudly.

Miss Shufflebottom sighed. "Posted just means Sabrina's parents were sent overseas to work," she said. "Carry on, Sabrina."

"Yes, my parents were *posted* overseas, because they have really cool jobs, but they wanted me to stay here with my uncle and go to a good school."

"But this school is a DUMP!"

That stopped me dead in my tracks. It wasn't the rude

language. I had heard mean words before, even at the Palace. The cooks and cleaners were always complaining and swearing in the kitchens, assuming no one could hear them. So I wasn't shocked about the rudeness. I *was* shocked that I'd been interrupted, twice. No one had ever interrupted me before. At the Palace, royals could talk for hours and everyone had to listen. But that horrid, greasy-haired, gum-sucking baby at the back of the class had interrupted me. Twice!

"Agatha, please, let's be kind today," mumbled Miss Shufflebottom.

My behaviour wasn't particularly regal, but I actually glared at my new teacher. No wonder she was lumbered with a name like Shufflebottom. She was a real shuffle-bottom, all weak and wobbly.

At the Palace, Miss Cruickshanks was known to have a cane for the other young royals. I'd never needed it. But we had all heard the rumours. The cane was a long, knotted stick full of splinters that had been passed from one Cruickshanks to another. My father and my grandfather had all feared the Cruickshanks Cane.

When I asked Daddy about it once, he giggled and said, "Oh yes, make sure you never get to meet the famous Cruickshanks Cane. It's a killer cane!"

So I knew not to mess with old Miss Quick-Pants. No matter how saggy and wrinkly she got, the old bat always had the legendary Cruickshanks Cane.

But this Shufflebottom had nothing, not even a booming voice.

"But it is a dump! It's rubbish! It's garbage! It's absolutely—"

And then she called the school something I simply refuse to repeat, even in a private autobiography that will be locked in my bedroom drawer. She leaned back on her chair and chewed the gum on the inside of her cheek.

"Agatha, please, we have spoken about this many times."

Miss Shufflebottom's voice had gone even softer and lighter. It was all tingly and gooey, like she was talking to a baby. She really was useless.

Agatha snarled at Miss Shufflebottom. "Spoke about what, Miss? You're the one who says we've got to express our feelings, right? Well, those are my feelings, Miss. This school is a dump and your classroom is a dump, right?"

And then she looked right at me.

Every head in the class swivelled from Agatha to me. It was like the audience of a tennis match at the Palace. Even Miss Shufflebottom looked at me. She probably didn't even realise she was looking at me. But I'm sure she was delighted. The class' attention had shifted from her to me. I didn't know what to say.

"Come on, new girl, don't be shy," Agatha shouted across the classroom. "Yeah, you, with the long hair and the pretty eyes, what do you think about this dump? Tell us the truth. Go on. Even this classroom is a smelly pile of dog poo."

"Well, maybe that's because you're sitting in it."

I heard the words fly across the classroom and realised they were mine. Daddy always said I was blessed and cursed with a tongue that was too fast for its own good.

Miss Shufflebottom's jaw dropped so low, I could see the silver and black fillings at the back of her teeth. There were three. She didn't eat enough fruit and vegetables.

And then I heard the laughing. Behind every desk, there was a student clutching his or her sides. They were really belly laughing, too. This wasn't that kind of polite smiling I always had to put on when one of my grandparents told an offensive joke, but the real thing. Charles was wiping tears from his eyes. Even Miss Shufflebottom might have let a quick smile slip from her lips.

In fact, I blame Miss Shufflebottom for what happened next.

I was sneaking a peek at her half-smile when my peripheral vision spotted something flying through the air. I know all about peripheral vision. Our ponies at the Palace all had peripheral vision. Their eyes were stuck on the sides of their heads so they could see sideways. I tried to look out the side of my head like one of the Palace ponies, but I wasn't fast enough.

A tiny, round brain flew towards me and hit me straight in the eye.

"Argh!" I shrieked. "I've been hit in the eye! I'm blind, Miss Shufflebottom, I'm blind!"

I must have really screamed because Miss Shufflebottom finally did some shuffling. She ran over and grabbed me by the shoulders. With one hand, she tilted my head back. Everything was blurry and scary. Through my stinging eyes, I saw her other hand coming towards my face.

"Argh! Argh! Argh! You're pulling out my eyeball!"

"It's not your eyeball," she said calmly. "It's just chewing gum. It's Agatha's chewing gum."

I was sobbing now. I didn't want to, not on my first day, but I couldn't stop myself.

"You see? I told you this place was a dump," said the girl I HATED more than any other person on the entire planet.

CHAPTER SEVEN

We were both sent to Miss Cannington's office. She was the headmistress. I wasn't scared. Not really. I knew what it was like to be really scared, properly scared. What was happening to my family back at the Palace, now that was scary.

This was just annoying.

The only person who looked totally terrified was Miss Shufflebottom. She had led us down the corridor in a hurry. I thought she was going to burst into tears outside the door.

"Are you going to come inside with us?" I whispered.

I had to whisper. My lip was quivering in a really weird way. My belly was flipping somersaults. I thought it was fear, at first, but then I realised it was anger. I wanted to smack the stinking gum-spitter beside me.

Naturally, Awful Agatha thought the whole thing was hilarious.

"Yeah, stay Miss," she said, grinning her ugly head off at Miss Shufflebottom. "It'll be a laugh with the old Cannibal."

"Be quiet, Agatha, really, not another word from you," Miss Shufflebottom hissed. "I'm sure I'll have to come back and see Miss Cannington later."

She knocked on the headmistress' door, pushed us into the office and left.

"Sit down," Miss Cannington muttered.

Miss Cannington had one of those soft voices of authority, rather like a royal voice. When she talked, others listened. She didn't shout because she didn't need to shout. She reminded me of my mother. Or at least I think she did. My mind was a muddle: Did Miss Cannington really remind me of Mummy or did I just really need Mummy because I'd been sent to Miss Cannington? I couldn't decide and didn't really want to. My eyes were still red and puffy from all that crying in the classroom.

We sat down. Even the brat beside me didn't argue.

Miss Cannington sat behind a large, polished desk. She wore those glasses without rims, the ones that try to look invisible. Her hair was far too short to be fashionable. She was in trousers and a long-sleeved shirt, like she was taking part in a competition to look like a man.

She took a deep breath and held it for so long I thought she was having a heart attack.

"Agatha, Agatha, Agatha," she eventually said, shaking her head.

She really did say the nasty girl's name three times. Perhaps Awful Agatha was training to be a witch and Miss Cannington was trying to break the spell.

"Why do you keep doing this to yourself?"

"I didn't do anything to myself, Miss."

Agatha grinned and nodded towards my eye, the one that had just been splattered by her disgusting gum. I felt an urge, like boiling water was rising from the pit of my stomach and racing towards my head. I clenched my fists beneath my seat, but what I really wanted to do was yank the little monster's greasy hair and flip her across Miss Cannington's polished desk.

But I didn't. Of course I didn't. Princesses do not punch members of the public, no matter how irritating they are. Uncle Ernie always reminded me of my duties during our taekwondo lessons at the Palace. *Never attack. Never retaliate. Always walk away.*

But that was easy for Uncle Ernie to say. He'd never been hit in the eye with a fat glob of gum.

"No, you never seem to do anything, do you, Agatha? And yet, you always end up in my office, telling me, yet again, that you didn't do anything. You must be the unluckiest girl in the world."

Miss Cannington sounded a bit like Uncle Ernie. He was sarcastic, too.

"I'm not saying nothing," Agatha said.

"No, you're not saying *anything*," Miss Cannington corrected. "If you're not saying nothing, then you're saying something. It's a double negative."

"Then I'm doubly negative not saying nothing."

That made me giggle. I couldn't help it. Awful Agatha sounded ridiculous. Now the headmistress and the little pest were both staring at me.

"Are you making fun of me?"

Agatha's eyes were so wide I could see the little red veins inside.

"No."

"Yes, you are. Don't make fun of the way I talk."

"I'm not."

"Do you think I'm stupid?"

"What? No."

"You think I'm stupid."

"I don't."

"If you think I'm stupid, I'll take you outside and —"

"Agatha, that's enough," Miss Cannington interrupted. "There's no need to show off."

"I'm not showing off. She's the one showing off. She made fun of me in class. She said I was disgusting. Now she's saying I'm stupid."

"I'm sure she didn't say any of those things, did you, Miss ..."

That annoyed me. The headmistress didn't even know my name. Where I'm from, every single person in the country knows my name. All right, I'm a princess, but that's not the point, is it? I hadn't joined Miss Cannington's rotten school on the first day of term. I arrived in the middle of term. I was the only one. Just me, Sabrina Parslowe, the new kid in class. The one with chewing gum hanging from her eyeball. The one sitting beside the spitting witch. She's only got one new name to remember, and she couldn't even do that.

"Sabrina," I mumbled. "My name is Sabrina Parslowe."

"Oh yes, of course. You only started this morning, didn't you?"

"Yes, Miss Cannington."

"And you're in my office already?"

"Yes, Miss Cannington."

"And why are you in my office already, Sabrina?"

I turned my head slightly, but I didn't want to look at her silly, smug face. I wasn't going to give her the satisfaction. I wanted to humiliate her. I wanted more than anything else in the world to tell Miss Cannington what really happened. But Uncle Ernie had already told me that little white lies are sometimes necessary to protect a bigger, more important truth. I had to sit back and become the invisible princess.

"I got very emotional, Miss Cannington," I said.

"I know you did. Miss Shufflebottom told me. She said there was an incident with some chewing gum. Isn't that right, Sabrina?"

Awful Agatha and I looked at each other. She grinned at me again. The mad girl actually *wanted* me to tell tales. That would make me the snitch, the blabbermouth, the classroom rat. And everyone hates a rat. I knew it would be pretty hard to remain incognito if I were the most hated girl in class. I could see that Awful Agatha already had that title and she was welcome to it.

Her dopey grin showed her teeth. They were crooked and chipped, like gravestones in a cemetery. And they were turning yellow. She didn't brush her teeth properly. What kind of girl didn't brush her teeth properly? I almost felt sorry for her. *Almost.* I'm not sure why.

"It was just a misunderstanding," I said. "Isn't that right, Agatha?"

Her smile vanished. Her face was half-terrified and half-confused. For the first time all morning, she was truly lost for words. I almost laughed, but my giggling had landed me in enough trouble for one day.

"Are you sure, Sabrina?"

Miss Cannington obviously wasn't convinced by my little white lie. I needed Awful Agatha to back me up.

"Yes, Miss Cannington. It's my first day, I've just moved to a new town, my parents are working overseas and I'm a little lost. So we just had a bit of a misunderstanding."

I nodded at Awful Agatha. She blinked and snapped out of her daze.

"Er, yeah, that's right. We had a miss ... a miss-undies ..."

"A misunderstanding," I added helpfully.

Awful Agatha's head suddenly flicked around like a cobra's tongue. "Are you making fun of me again?"

"What? No."

"Yeah, you are. You're making fun of me because I can't say your big, fancy words."

"I'm not."

"I think Sabrina is simply saying that there was a little confusion between the two of you," Miss Cannington interrupted.

"Yes, it was probably a little inconsiderate on my part," I said.

Now Miss Cannington was staring at me. "Inconsiderate? Misunderstanding? How old are you, Sabrina?"

"Er, eleven, Miss Cannington."

"Hmm. You're a bright little thing, aren't you?"

"She's an idiot," Awful Agatha muttered.

"That's enough, Agatha," Miss Cannington said, but she was still staring at me, as if she found me fascinating or something. "Sabrina? Sabrina Parslowe, right? I must find your file and read up on your last school."

"No, no, it wasn't the school. It was, well, I had some extra tuition classes at the pala ... pala ... place ... at the place I lived before."

"At the pala, pala, place? She even talks like an idiot," Awful Agatha said.

Miss Cannington ignored her. "Well, Sabrina, I'm all for extra education and study after school, but do remember that all work and no play makes Jack a dull boy."

"Who's Jack?" Awful Agatha asked.

Miss Cannington smiled. "Never mind Jack. I want you to shake hands and make up. Let's call it a misunderstanding and move on."

I held out my hand. The little weasel hesitated.

"Come on, Agatha, I haven't got all day," Miss Cannington said.

We shook hands, but Awful Agatha pulled her hand away really quickly, as if my fingers were all covered in bogeys.

Miss Cannington sent us back to class, but as soon as we were in the corridor, Awful Agatha grabbed my shoulder and spun me around. I bit my lip to stop myself from sweeping her legs away.

"Why did you do that?" she growled.

"Do what?"

"Make up all that stuff to get me out of trouble."

"I don't know. I had to, I suppose."

She looked down at her shoes. They were scuffed and muddy and one of the soles was cracking.

"No one's ever been nice to me before," she mumbled.

Then she took a step towards me and peered right into my eyes.

"I'm gonna get you for that."

CHAPTER EIGHT

Little Charles followed me around for the rest of the day. He was kind of sweet and annoying at the same time. He was also a bit of a midget. He looked up at me whenever he spoke, which was all the time.

"Miss Shufflebottom said I have to look after you, show you where all the different classes are," he said, as we made our way to the canteen.

I didn't believe him. He was telling one of those white lies, but I didn't really mind. In fact, I was starting to enjoy his company, sort of.

Charles was different, in a pathetic, harmless kind of way. Back at the Palace, my royal cousins and all the other princes, dukes and earls who visited were all loud and irritating. These boys always talked about the goals they'd scored in hockey or the fences they'd jumped in equestrian. They didn't tell little white lies either. They told enormous whoppers.

Charles was the opposite. He mostly told the truth about himself when he really should have told more lies.

"I'm rubbish at football," he said.

"Ok," I replied.

"And rugby, I'm even more rubbish at rugby," he continued.

"Really?"

"Yeah, I'm rubbish at all sports. In fact, there was one time when we were jumping on the trampoline. I lost my balance, fell off the trampoline and landed on my head."

"Is that why you're so short?"

"Yes. I used to be one of the tallest boys in the class. And then I fell off the trampoline."

"And landed on your head?"

"Exactly."

I looked Charles up and down. He really was short.

"How many times did you fall on your head?" I wondered.

"Only once. Don't be sarky," he said. "It was a really big fall, ok? It stopped me being as tall as them."

Charles nodded towards a gang of boys heading towards us. They whooped and pushed each other as they banged their trays down on our table in the canteen.

"They're all really good at football," Charles said.

"Is that important?" I asked.

"It is here."

I had no idea why he was going on about the football talents of strangers I didn't know.

"Are you good at football?" he asked. "I mean, did you play football in your old school? I bet you were the captain of the team, right?"

"No, I didn't play football."

"You'd be really good at football."

Charles was trying to flatter me. He probably felt sorry for me because of the Awful Agatha business. But really, she was the least of my problems. If nothing else, Charles stopped me thinking about family stuff that I didn't really want to think about.

"I played hockey and lacrosse at my last school," I said. "And I was pretty useless at both."

"Blimey, your school must have been really posh. We never play hockey here and I've never even heard of lacrosse. Is that a foreign game? Is it like the French version of noughts and crosses?"

Charles put on a European accent that was neither French nor German. It was just terrible. "I vant to play ze game of la cross with you, yah," he said.

I started giggling. It felt really good. The stingy, stabbing pains that had poked me in the stomach since Miss Cannington's office floated away.

"Don't laugh. That's a brilliant accent."

"Yeah, but what accent is it?"

"Tis la accent of ze European peoples, mon amigo!"

"Sounds like the accent of Dracula."

I laughed again and maybe for too long this time. Charles scrunched up his face.

"You don't have to sit with me in the canteen, you know. I don't mind. I'm used to it. I can sit in the corner and do my quizzes."

"What kind of quizzes?"

"You don't want to know."

"No, I do really."

"Are you sure?"

"Yes, Charlie."

"Can you call me Charles? Where I come from, Charlie sounds really common."

"Where I come from, Charles sounds really common."

"But Charles sounds like the name of a king."

"Exactly."

Charles looked confused. "Eh? How can a king's name be common?"

"Tell me about your quizzes," I said quickly.

Charles flipped open his laptop. He was giddy with excitement. I suspected that no one had asked to see his quizzes before.

"Well, they're not so much quizzes, more like murder mysteries."

"What?"

Charles must have noticed my face change.

"No, no, no, they're not violent or anything," he insisted. "They're maths and English comprehension quizzes, but instead of just doing really boring sums and sentences, they give you murder mysteries to solve."

Charles pointed at a cartoon character on his screen. It was lying face down and covered in blood.

"You see, this one: There were 107 suspects, but the police found a blonde hair on the weapon and 38 of the 107 suspects had blonde hair. Get it?"

"You subtract 38 from 107 and eliminate the other 69 suspects."

"Wow, you did that without a calculator."

Charles flicked the page on his screen.

"Or there's this one: A queen has been kidnapped inside her castle. She has 28 members of staff inside the castle."

I pulled a face. "Yeah, I get it."

"And 15 of them were in the kitchen when the queen was kidnapped."

"Can we talk about something else now?"

"And 5 of them were in the garage where the rope was taken."

"Please stop now."

"But the queen's bloody dressing gown was found in the bathroom and ..."

"CHARLES, WOULD YOU PLEASE SHUT UP!"

The noisy boys at the other end of the table stopped talking. In fact, the entire canteen fell silent. I saw the blood drain from poor Charles' face. He kept blinking at me. I knew straightaway what that meant. Since my parents sent me away, I was always blinking in public places, anything to stop the waterworks.

"Who was that?"

I recognised that voice. Even though it was my first day at school, it was already a familiar voice. A shadow appeared across my lunch. I looked up and found myself peering into Miss Cannington's flaming nostrils. At least they were clean. She obviously picked her nose regularly, just like I did. My parents said I wasn't to use my fingers to hunt around for bogeys in public. But Uncle Ernie didn't mind me having a quick nose pick as long as I was discreet.

What the public eye doesn't see, the private princess gets away with.

Uncle Ernie always said that, usually after I'd caught him pulling the biggest, hairiest and most disgusting bogeys from his wrinkled hooter.

"Oh, it's you," said Miss Cannington's nostrils. I still couldn't see past the nose on the end of her face.

"It's Sabrina, isn't it?"

"Yes, Miss Cannington," I replied.

"You are making quite the first impression, aren't you?"

"Yes, Miss Cannington."

"Who's picking you up from school today?"

"My uncle, Miss Cannington."

"Maybe I could have a chat with him at the school gates."

"Yes, Miss Cannington."

Uncle Ernie had repeated his firm instructions all weekend. *Do not get into trouble. Do not cause a scene. Do not draw attention to yourself.* On my first day, I had gotten into trouble, twice. I had caused a scene with a weepy-eyed Charles. And now, I had the full attention of every kid in the school canteen.

Uncle Ernie was going to kill me.

CHAPTER NINE

I had hoped that Miss Cannington would let me walk to the school gates on my own. Fat chance. She escorted me from the classroom, along the corridor and out into the playground.

"I wouldn't want you to get lost going home on your first day," she said.

I wasn't a total dimwit. She didn't want me to run away.

Clearly, this lousy school produced loads of lousy students like Awful Agatha and Miss Cannington thought I was another one. Obviously, she couldn't see through her rimless glasses properly. Maybe Awful Agatha was right. Maybe Miss Cannington really was a nasty, old cannibal, chewing on little children all through the day and then spitting them out at home time.

The old Cannibal definitely needed her eyes tested if she saw me as the new brat of the class. Why do teachers like Miss Shufflebottom and Miss Cannington waste so much time on real devils like Awful Agatha and ignore the rest of us? It should be the other way round, right? They should spend more time on the quieter students. We're the ones who always get forgotten about. If these upside-down teachers noticed us a bit more, they'd work out that we were just as important as the nasty brats.

And then, they'd get their facts straight.

And then, they wouldn't be leading well-behaved students like me through the playground.

All the other kids stared at me. Some of the parents did, too, but I wasn't bothered. I didn't care. People stared at me all the time back at home. Only one person worried me at that moment.

And he looked furious.

Even though the playground was crammed with children running around like lunatics, Uncle Ernie spotted me in the crowd. At royal events back at the Palace, he followed me and Mum and Dad everywhere. His eyes were like lasers. He said that was part of his job as the Palace's handyman, but I wasn't born yesterday. He always wore an earpiece, too. Handymen didn't need earpieces to paint walls and fix floorboards. He said he was listening to music, but I knew he was really listening to other *handymen* who worked at the Palace.

They wore earpieces, too. They weren't handymen either.

Uncle Ernie wasn't wearing an earpiece at the school gates, but his laser-like eyes still tracked my every move. He noticed the snooty headmistress beside me, prodding me towards him.

He was not smiling.

"This is Uncle Ernie," I mumbled, preferring to look at my shoes.

"Ah yes, I believe we spoke on the phone. I'm Miss Cannington," she said, holding out her hand.

They shook hands, but I could tell that Uncle Ernie didn't really want to.

"Oh, yes, when I registered her for the school," he replied.

"Yes, well, I was going to invite you in for a chat. I think it's important that we maintain a relationship with all our parents. Or, in this case, *guardians*."

I didn't like the way she said *guardians*. It was kind of sarcastic, a bit like the way I sometimes say *whatever* to Uncle Ernie when I don't agree with him. He hates that. I noticed his eyebrow go up as Miss Cannington spoke. He didn't like the way she said *guardians* either.

"Yes, I'm her Uncle Ernie," he said, putting on a really fake smile.

Miss Cannington examined his face, as if she were looking for something.

"Yes, yes, I can see a faint resemblance."

"Yes, we both have long, brown hair, don't we?"

"Ha ha, quite."

Miss Cannington laughed far too loudly for a joke I didn't get.

"And what can I do for you, Miss Cannington?" Uncle Ernie asked, in that smooth voice he uses to calm strangers down at the Palace. "Don't tell me little Sabrina here is in trouble on her first day?"

"No, of course not. It's not so much trouble as it is a tricky period of adjustment, perhaps, which is completely understandable. A new town, a new school and a new family."

"Just a new school and town," Uncle Ernie said firmly. "Not a new family."

He smiled at me and I smiled back, which was probably

for the best as my eyes were stinging in the corners. Why do people always want to go on and on about my family? I have no interest whatsoever in talking about their families. In fact, I don't want to talk about anyone's family, ever. I find the subject just, so, *whatever*. When I hear the word, my belly tightens and my eyes go all blurry. Why is everyone in this nosey new school so cruel and evil?

Even Uncle Ernie was fed up with all the family talk. I could see that Miss Cannington's comments were getting on his nerves.

"I was waiting outside the birthing suite on the day this little girl was born," he said.

And then he winked at me, which made my insides turn all mushy like mashed potato.

"I've seen Sabrina on almost every day of her life."

Miss Cannington looked uncomfortable. "You must be a very close family."

"We were," Uncle Ernie replied. "We are."

"That's wonderful. Then I'm sure you'll understand how difficult it must be for Sabrina to settle into a new school."

"Why? Has she done anything wrong?"

"Well, there was a little *incident* with a girl in her class."

"An incident? Seriously?" I snapped. "She threw chewing gum into my eyeball! She rolled it up in her disgusting saliva and then spat it into my face!"

For some reason, my mouth had sprung a leak. All of this angry stuff came gushing out of me like a geyser in one of those American national parks. I couldn't stop shouting.

"Where I come from, that Agatha would've been dragged from the drawing room! Where I come from, old Quick-Pants would've slapped the brat with her knobbly cane and locked her in the kitchens with the chefs!"

For a good few seconds, the two grown-ups just stood there with their mouths agape. I could see their squidgy, pink tonsils.

"Sabrina, what are you doing?" Uncle Ernie muttered finally.

Miss Cannington's eyes had narrowed to slits. "Knobbly cane, quick pants, drawing room and chefs in kitchens ... what was the name of your last school again?"

"She was home-schooled mostly," Uncle Ernie said, really quickly. "Her parents moved around so much with their work, that it made it easier. Plus, they are very private people."

Miss Cannington leaned closer. "They're not, like, famous celebrities, are they?"

Uncle Ernie touched his nose with his finger. "Ah, that would be telling, wouldn't it?"

"No, I completely understand. We'll say no more about it," Miss Cannington said. Her cheeks were turning red.

"Actually, we have a bit of a history with famous people here. I believe that one of our parents once played Miss Hannigan in *Annie*," she continued.

"In the movie?" Uncle Ernie asked.

"No, in our local theatre. It's a lovely small theatre, on the edge of town, next to the recycling centre. So have no fear, we have experience in handling famous parents with the utmost discretion."

"That's good to know."

"And what do you do, Mr ..."

"It's Parslowe, too, but please call me Ernie."

Miss Cannington blushed for the second time. "Ernie, right. And what do you do, Ernie? Do you work locally?"

"Well, Miss Cannington ... I'm sorry, is it Miss or Mrs?"

"It's Ms or Miss, or anything really," she said, rolling her eyes.

"Really? That surprises me."

"Why?"

"Well, I just figured a smart lady like yourself would be happily married."

Miss Cannington now looked like she'd been baked in the sun for a week. "Oh, Mr Parslowe, please."

"Ernie."

"Ernie, sorry Ernie, yes, well, you know how it is. I'm married to my work. I love my students," Miss Cannington said, putting her arm around me, which made me want to vomit. "And I've got my cats. I adore my three cats. So I just don't have the time for, you know."

"Ah, you're still young."

"Er, probably not as young as you'd think."

"No, I figure you're in your late thirties, but still look younger."

Miss Cannington squealed like a rusty door hinge.

"Ooh, Ernie, ha ha, you're far too kind. I wish I were still in my thirties. I'm actually in my for ... for ... for what it's worth, we're probably much closer in age than you think."

"Never. When you walked over, I thought you were one of the students."

I thought I was going to be sick.

"Ha ha, one of the students," said Miss Cannington, adjusting her hair. "Your uncle certainly has a sense of humour."

"Just saying what I see, Miss Cannington. Just saying what I see. So, what's the problem with Sabrina?"

"Oh, it's nothing really, first-day blues. We settled the incident with the chewing gum and she got a little enthusiastic, shall we say, with another student in the canteen. That's all. Perhaps you can have a chat at home later."

"Oh, we most certainly will, Miss Cannington."

"And maybe you could pop into my office one day for a chat."

Miss Cannington beamed at Uncle Ernie. I could almost taste the vomit at the back of my throat.

"I'd like that," Uncle Ernie replied, already dragging me away.

"It's a date then, ha ha," she cried.

Miss Cannington giggled like a little girl all the way across the playground.

"Do you really think she looks like a student?" I wondered.

"Only if I keep my eyes closed," Uncle Ernie said gruffly. "Get in the van. Now!"

CHAPTER TEN

I was in no mood for my taekwondo lesson and neither was Uncle Ernie. I could tell. He was frowning too much. He had at least five squiggly lines running across his forehead. He had turned our dining room into a temporary *dojang*. There were blue gymnastics mats all over the floor and he'd bought a punching bag while I was at school. He had even squeezed in a metal bar across the door frame for chin-ups. But I didn't want to do any chin-ups either.

I knew what Uncle Ernie was trying to do, of course. I'm not daft. He was trying to make this tiny house look like our old home. But this wasn't home. My family wasn't here.

"Hit the pads, come on, roundhouse kicks, five on each side," he said.

He was wearing a leather pad on each arm. He wore them to prevent bruises from my epic roundhouse kicks. One time, I spun around so fast that I lost my balance slightly and kicked him between the legs. He bent over and actually started crying. That's how awesome my flying kicks are.

I flicked one kick, but I couldn't really be bothered. My foot smashed into Uncle Ernie's bony elbow.

"Ow!" he howled in pain. "You should be aiming your kicks much higher!"

He rubbed his reddening elbow. He'd have a bruise in the morning.

"Sorry, Uncle Ernie, but I can't concentrate. I'm really stressed."

"Oh, come on, Sabrina. What have you got to be stressed about?"

"Er, well, there's the fact that I can't see my parents because the people in our country want to get rid of our royal family. That kinda sucks, you know? I lost all my old friends. That really sucks. I had to leave the Palace for a house in a street where all the houses look the same. That sucks big time. I've got a dumb headmistress who thinks I'm a loud-mouthed bully when everyone at the school knows that Awful Agatha is the real bully. And she hates my guts. And I hate her guts. And I'm sorry I kicked you in the elbow. But I wish your elbow had been her fat, greasy head."

"Hey, what have I told you about taekwondo?"

"Yes, I know. It's only for self-defence. I'm not really going to kick her in the head."

"Good. Well, that's something at least. Let's try some punching."

I had told Uncle Ernie another little white lie. I knew it was a little white lie as soon as I started throwing punches. I imagined that the black pads really were Agatha's fat head. So I punched. And I punched. And I kept on punching until the sweat poured down my face.

"Aiyah!" I roared, as my final punch made Uncle Ernie slip backwards on the blue mats.

"All right, that's enough punching, tiger. You're not the only one who's had a stressful day, you know."

"Look, I said I was sorry about getting into trouble at school."

"It's not that. It's this!"

Uncle Ernie led me into the living room. He had not one, not two, but three laptops spread across a cluttered table. There were different coloured cables, all twisted and knotted and running all over the place. They looked like the veins in Uncle Ernie's legs.

"What's all this for?" I asked.

"Chaos, my girl. That's what all this is for. Do you know what I've been doing on these computers?"

"Playing Farm Heroes?"

"No, not Farm Heroes. I have been setting up a website for The Susan Fanshawe Home Schooling Centre."

"Ooh, what's that?"

"It's where you went to school before you moved here."

"But I was schooled at the Palace by old Quick-Pants."

"No, Sabrina Valence was schooled at the Palace. Sabrina Parslowe was schooled in a made-up place by the lovely Susan Fanshawe."

Uncle Ernie clicked on one of the laptop screens and a black and white photograph of a large lady with a hairy wart on the end of her nose popped up.

"Ugh, she doesn't look like a teacher."

"It doesn't matter. She isn't real. It's a composite photo."

"Yeah. She looks like compost."

"Not compost. Composite, which means she was made up from lots of little bits of other people's photos."

"Well, why did you give her a hairy wart?"

"I didn't have long, did I? I've got to come up with something in case your headmistress starts playing detective on the Internet."

"You said I was home-schooled!"

"Only because you started going on about the Palace chefs. You're supposed to be a simple girl from a small town. You don't have Palace chefs."

I scrolled through the pages of the website. There were comments from other parents and students, all saying what a fantastic teacher this Susan Fanshawe was.

"If she's such a brilliant, creative teacher, why does she have such a boring name? She should've come up with something better than The Susan Fanshawe Home Schooling Centre."

"Oh I'm sorry, did you not hear me properly just now. I DIDN'T HAVE ENOUGH TIME! I'm not trying to win the website of the year award!"

"Well, you wouldn't with this."

A sixth squiggly line appeared on Uncle Ernie's forehead. I decided not to make fun of his fake website anymore.

"The colours are really pretty though," I said.

Uncle Ernie sighed. "Thank you. I was rather pleased with the colour scheme."

I clicked on the "Contact" page and panicked.

"Uncle Ernie, you've messed up, look! You've put in an

email address and a phone number. Miss Cannington might try and call Susan Fanshawe and her hairy wart."

Uncle Ernie grinned. "She can't."

"Why not?"

"Susan Fanshawe is dead."

Uncle Ernie clicked on another website. In big, bold scary letters, the word "OBITUARY" stretched across the top of the page. There was the same black and white photograph of Susan Fanshawe and her humongous hairy wart, and beside it, some text explaining that she'd recently died.

Suddenly, my throat was itchy. I was worried that my eyes were about to sting.

"But that's ... so sad," I sniffed. "How did she die?"

"She was run over by a drunken hamster."

"Really?"

"No! She's not a real person!"

"Yah, but did you have to kill her?"

Uncle Ernie threw his arms in the air. "How did I kill her? She didn't exist in the first place! She's a fake photograph. It's fake news!"

"Yeah, but lots of people believe fake news."

"Then let them believe in Susan Fanshawe's death! Let them wear black armbands! Let's have a national Susan Fanshawe Day!"

"Ah, that's a good idea. Then her family can remember her."

"What family? She hasn't got a family! I made her up! She's a figment of my imagination, the solution to our latest problem, the only response I had to another emergency situation, the only thing I could do after we told your crazy headmistress with too many cats that you were home-schooled."

"Miss Cannington does have a lot of cats," I agreed.

Uncle Ernie took a deep breath.

"Anyway, it's done now. Let's just think about what we say. In fact, let's just say as little as possible, ok? No more slip-ups. Let's not reveal anything else about who we are, what we did or where we live, ok?"

And then, the doorbell rang.

I knew straightaway that we had a problem, especially when Uncle Ernie's bulging eyes looked like they were going to fly across the living room like ping pong balls.

I didn't even know we had a doorbell.

No one was supposed to know where we lived.

CHAPTER ELEVEN

Uncle Ernie told me to hide in the living room. I was always hiding. My life was turning into a never-ending game of hide-and-seek, but I had no one to play with. Well, I had my Uncle Ernie, but he was constantly making me do annoying stuff that I didn't want to do, like hide in my own house.

So I ignored him. As he left to open the front door, moaning under his breath, I followed him into the corridor. I was on my tiptoes the whole time, gliding along in my socks. Uncle Ernie had taught me to move silently during our taekwondo lessons.

"Yes," said Uncle Ernie, peering through the tiniest crack in the door. I craned my head, but I couldn't see a thing over his shoulder.

"I'm sorry, you must be mistaken," Uncle Ernie continued. "I live alone."

He tried to close the door, but a foot jammed itself in the gap at the bottom. The foot was brave, but small and stupid.

No one messed with Uncle Ernie. He had so many different skills for a handyman. So I knew he wasn't bothered about a tiny foot in the doorway. I was more worried about the foot being snapped off and the intruder hopping home with a soggy sock filled with blood.

"I wouldn't leave your foot in the door if I were you," Uncle Ernie warned. "I have a really big dog, a German Shepherd called Nibbler. He likes to nibble on the toes of children, particularly small boys."

I heard a faint whimper on the other side of the door.

"I don't care what you saw, young man, no one lives here but me. Are you going to leave? No? Ok, it's up to you."

Uncle Ernie turned back and whistled. "Ok, Nibbler, here boy! I've got five juicy toes, just for you. Come on, boy! Come and eat some cheesy feet!"

There was a kind of yelp behind the front door. It sounded pathetic, but familiar.

"Look, I don't care if you're Charlie, Charles or a King Charles Spaniel, you're not coming in."

Without thinking, I ran down the corridor and flung the door open. Little Charles stood on the doorstep. He was shaking. His cheeks were salmon-pink. He threw his hands over his eyes.

"No, Nibbler, no! Don't eat my feet! They're small and squishy and I've always got sock fluff between my toes."

"Ew, that's disgusting," I said.

Charles peeked through a crack in his fingers. "Sabrina? Is that you?"

"Of course it's me."

Charles pulled his hands away. "What about Nibbler? And what about my toes? And why do you have a toe-eating dog?"

"We don't have a toe-eating dog. We just have Uncle Ernie."

"Your uncle eats toes?"

"No one eats toes in this house. My Uncle Ernie was just messing around, right, Uncle Ernie?"

Uncle Ernie said nothing. He quietly growled so I nudged him in the ribs.

"We don't have a dog in the house, do we, Uncle Ernie?"

Uncle Ernie sighed. "No, young Charles, we do not have a dog in the house."

Charles smiled for the first time. And then, Uncle Ernie leaned forward and whispered in his ear.

"We keep our toe-eating dog in the garden."

Charles screamed and ran off down the garden path.

"No, wait, come back," I shouted. "We don't have a dog. Uncle Ernie is being silly again. Why would we have such a deadly dog? Come in and see for yourself."

Uncle Ernie looked like he might have a heart attack. "What? We can't have guests. We're not ready to have guests. The house is a mess."

"Charles won't care about that stuff. Will you, Charles?"

The shivering titch hesitated at first, but then slowly returned along our garden path. "No, I won't mind, really. You should see my house."

"But you've got to do your homework," Uncle Ernie insisted.

"It's her first day at school," said Charles. "She hasn't got any homework."

Uncle Ernie's head swivelled around so fast I thought it might spin off like a bottle top. "Are you a detective?"

"No, sir."

"Are you sure? You seem to have my niece under surveillance. I presume you followed her home from school?"

"Yes, sir."

Charles couldn't look Uncle Ernie in the eye. I felt a bit sorry for him. I mean, he was still weak and feeble and far too obsessed with maths and puzzles, but he looked like he needed someone. I didn't have much time for maths and puzzles. But I knew that feeling about needing someone.

"But we came home in a van," Uncle Ernie continued. "Did you run after us? Are you training for the Olympics?"

"No. I told my Mum that I had taken Sabrina's reading book by mistake and we followed you in our car."

"Wow, so you're an expert in surveillance and a master of deception, too."

"No, I'm not."

"So why are you here then?"

Charles looked straight at me. He sniffed hard and wiped his eyes.

"You seemed really upset at the canteen. I wanted to say that I was sorry if I did that."

I suddenly felt weird. The insides of my belly flapped and fluttered, just as they had since I'd been forced to leave my parents. That fluttering felt like a load of bees and wasps bouncing around and stinging me all at once, but this fluttering felt like floating butterflies. It was fuzzy and different. It felt good.

Without thinking, I grabbed Charles by the collar of his ugly green blazer and dragged him into the house.

CHAPTER TWELVE

Uncle Ernie's head seemed ready to explode. His wrinkled forehead now had more lines than an exercise book. He didn't know whether to glare at poor Charles or me. I decided to break the ice.

"This is Charles," I said.

"I know that," grumbled Uncle Ernie.

"He is my new friend at my new school. In fact, he's my only friend at my new school. In fact, he's my only friend in my new town. In fact, he's the only person who's been kind to me since we moved from—"

"Yes, yes, yes, I get it," interrupted Uncle Ernie, holding his hands in the air. "You're right. I suppose it won't kill anyone to have a friend come and visit."

Charles looked relieved.

"At least I won't kill anyone," Uncle Ernie muttered.

Charles stopped looking relieved.

"I'm only joking," Uncle Ernie said, chuckling to himself. "Would you like a drink, Charles?"

"Yes, please. My mother says I can only drink fresh fruit juice, like a fruit with lots of vitamin C. Can I have some orange juice?"

Uncle Ernie gritted his teeth. "Certainly, sir."

As he headed for the kitchen, Charles called after him,

"Could I have some ice with it please, maybe four or five chunks of ice?"

Uncle Ernie stopped and muttered, "Back home, I'd chop you up and feed you to the dogs."

"What did you say?" asked Charles.

"I said, 'Back home, I'd chop up food for the dogs,'" Uncle Ernie shouted back.

"But you said you don't have any dogs," said a rather nervous Charles.

"I know," replied Uncle Ernie. "It's such a shame."

"Ignore him," I said. "He's always making lame jokes. Come on, I'll show you around the house."

By the time I'd finished the tour of my new home I was exhausted. Charles asked so many questions. For a boy who spent so much time with his nose stuck inside a book, he wasn't very bright. He wondered why young girls would learn taekwondo. Why wouldn't young girls learn taekwondo? How would they defend themselves in a world that was mostly ruled by men? It seemed perfectly obvious to me. But Charles didn't like sports or exercise that much. He didn't have much time for sporty boys, let alone sporty girls.

"I've just never seen a girl do this stuff before," he said, as I showed him the crash mats and punching bags that we used in our taekwondo sessions. "It's weird."

"Well, it's not weird where I come from, ok? It's totally normal."

Charles pushed a punching bag and didn't move out of its

way when the punching bag swung back and whacked him in the nose.

"So where did you come from, then? Was it a rough neighbourhood?" Charles asked, rubbing his red nose.

"Yeah, I suppose so."

"Well, you won't have to do any of this karate chopping here."

"It's taekwondo."

"Whatever."

"Is your nose ok? It's very red."

"My nose is fine," Charles said, but he was still massaging the swollen bit above his nostrils. "Now you're living here, in a nice place, you can do normal things for girls."

"Like what?"

"I don't know, cheerleading? Loads of girls do cheerleading on TV."

"What's cheerleading?"

"Cheerleading? You know, you wave pom-poms and cheer all the boys when they score a goal or something. That's what girls like you normally do."

"What do you mean, girls like me?"

Charles almost lost his voice. "You know, girls who look like, you know ... like ... when you're in the mirror, you must know that ... ok, let's say our school does a *Cinderella* musical, right? You wouldn't be able to play the Fairy Godmother because you're too young, right? You wouldn't be able to play the Ugly Sisters because, you know, you're not that ugly. So you'd have to play Cinderella because she's, you know ..."

"Kind?"

"No."

"Brave?"

"No."

"Good at sweeping the floor?"

"No. Just forget it."

"And who would you play? The pumpkin?"

"No, I wouldn't be in the musical. They wouldn't let me be in the musical. I'd be told to do something really boring on these."

Charles pointed at the three laptops in Uncle Ernie's messy living room. There were cables and whirring boxes and modems with flashing lights everywhere.

"Why do you have three laptops anyway?" Charles asked.

"Uncle Ernie needs them for his job."

"You said he was a handyman."

Charles crouched over one of the screens. "What's a Mulakating?"

I had never run so fast. I was across the office and around the desk like a cheetah sprinting across the Serengeti.

"Sorry, but Uncle Ernie likes to keep his work private."

"Oh, right. But what's a Mulakating?"

"Wow, you really ask a lot of questions," I said. "A Mulakating is a ... well, it's a kind of ..."

"It's a monkey wrench."

Uncle Ernie appeared from nowhere. For once, I was pleased to see him.

"What's a monkey wrench?" Charles asked.

I liked Charles, but he was turning into a right busybody.

"A monkey wrench is an adjustable spanner," Uncle Ernie said, as he went around the desk switching off each laptop. "A Mulakating is just my silly nickname for a monkey wrench. I use it to fix toilets—really blocked, smelly toilets, the kind of toilets that make you throw up, the kind of toilets that are filled with piles of steaming, horrible gooey stuff, the kind of toilets that can melt the skin on your face and ..."

"Yes, yes, all right, Uncle Ernie."

"Oh, I was going to get a monkey wrench and show the inquisitive Charles here how to unblock a really disgusting toilet. Would you like to see, Charles?"

Charles winced and turned almost as green as his school blazer.

"No, it's ok. I have to go home now."

"Fair enough, young man. But if you ever want to see all the squidgy stuff that swirls around in a blocked toilet, we'll have a nice glass of freshly-squeezed orange juice with four or five chunks of ice and then I'll get my monkey wrench."

Charles hurried towards the front door. When he reached the garden path, he said, "Your uncle is weird."

"I know," I said. "But he looks after me."

Charles smiled. "I know. So I'll see you at school tomorrow."

"Definitely."

Now I was smiling.

Charles closed the garden gate behind him. "Sabrina, can I ask you a question?"

"You ask more questions than Miss Shufflebottom!"

Charles cleared his throat. "It's about your living room."

"Yeah?"

"Why is there a photo of you standing in front of a castle and wearing a crown?"

CHAPTER THIRTEEN

My little white lies were seriously getting out of hand. Even that's a little white lie because I wasn't even telling little white lies anymore. I was telling huge, ginormous, pitch black lies that were getting harder and harder to keep up with. First, there was my surname and my backstory. I didn't even know what a backstory was until Uncle Ernie told me. A backstory is a past life about a character, all of the stuff she has done before today. Well, my backstory was all made up to hide the royal family thing.

But Charles wasn't convinced. That was obvious. He'd have to be a bit thick if he believed Uncle Ernie's nonsense about Mulakating being a nickname for a monkey wrench. It's already a stupid name for a spanner. Who gives a monkey wrench a nickname anyway? My Uncle Ernie, that's who. So now I had to remember my name, my backstory and the most ridiculous name in the history of ridiculous names for a monkey wrench.

And, thanks to Charles and his big nose poking around my private photographs, I had to come up with the gold medal of little white lies.

Luckily, I'd had all night to sleep on it. Not that I get much sleep, not since I left Mum and Dad. It's a time to think and I don't want to think. When my bedroom is dark,

I can see their faces, smiling at me, but I can't smile back. My eyes start stinging and I run to the toilet. But at least my non-stop trips to the bathroom had given me enough time to think about Charles spotting that royal photograph outside the Palace.

"It was a trip to a theme park," I whispered to him the next day in Miss Shufflebottom's class.

I knew straightaway that he needed further convincing.

"I know it's not Disneyland," I added. "It was in a strange, faraway place with a funny name."

Charles leaned over and said, "What, like, Scotland?"

I did say that he was a bit thick.

"No, not Scotland. But it might have been one of those countries in Europe with really long names and loads of castles and mountains."

"Oh, like *The Sound of Music*?"

"That's not a country. That's a movie."

"I know that. I mean the place where they made the movie, that looked a bit like where you were in your family photo."

"How long did you stare at the photo?"

"Not long, but I really like *The Sound of Music*."

Charles was a peculiar boy. For a moment, I thought he was going to start singing.

"It's not from *The Sound of Music*," I whispered, not realising that my voice was getting louder. "And it's not in Scotland either. It was just a place we went on holiday and I dressed up as a princess because I used to like dressing up as princesses. All little girls like dressing up as princesses, you know."

Charles stared at me for what seemed like ages. "Yes, but you're not a little girl in that photo. And you still like dressing up as a princess. That's worse than still liking *The Sound of Music*."

"WHO LIKES *THE SOUND OF MUSIC?*"

Everyone stopped talking. Even Miss Shufflebottom stopped scribbling on the whiteboard and turned around.

It was Agatha. It was the awful, smelly, awful, nasty, awful, vicious, awful Agatha.

She had spun around like a slimy snake to face Charles and me.

His head was already leaking. Little drops of sweat trickled down his spectacles. He knew he was in trouble. He knew he had broken one of the classroom rules.

There are hundreds of classroom rules and everyone knows them. They are all the same. Boys and girls can't say they miss their parents, not at school. They can't call them "Mummy" or "Daddy" either, not at our age. And never slip up and call the teacher "Mummy" or "Daddy", not if you're older than seven or eight. The little ones can get away with it. Sometimes, they even sound cute. But if a grown-up kid calls a teacher that, that's it. Life will not be worth living for the rest of the year.

Then there are the everyday rules. Young kids can bring their toys to school, but the really big kids never bring toys to school. That's just embarrassing. Phones, yes. Toys, no.

Boys and girls can play together when they're little, but not when they're our age, unless they want to start all sorts of silly rumours. Even Charles knows he's taking a risk sitting with me in class, but Miss Shufflebottom told him to so he has an excuse.

Little girls are allowed to dress up as princesses, but older girls can't.

Wearing a princess' dress at our school is like having an accident in our underwear. It's an EPIC disaster, the worst nightmare EVER.

You. Just. Don't. Do. It.

My situation is even more frustrating because I *am* a princess. I'm not playing pretend. This is who I really am. I have every right to wear the frilly, fluffy dresses and the shiny crowns and tiaras that little girls wear at birthday parties.

But I'm not a princess here. I'm just a grown-up girl with no friends who likes to dress up as a princess, according to Charles. That's like peeing my knickers in the school playground. If the other students found out, I'd be finished.

But I also knew that if there's one thing worse than being a big girl in a princess dress, it's being a big boy who likes *The Sound of Music*. It's just another one of those stupid, sexist classroom rules that make no sense. If Awful Agatha ever found out that Charles loves to sing and dance around his living room, his life would be so miserable. I had to do something to save him.

"I do!" I blurted out.

As usual, the greasy goblin was chewing her disgusting gum. She blew a bright, pink bubble that stretched towards my face. It popped just in front of my nose, making me blink.

All the other girls around her started laughing, only because they didn't want her to start picking on them. I could tell they weren't really her friends. Girls like Awful Agatha didn't have real friends.

"So you like *The Sound of Music*, eh?" she hissed.

"Er, yeah, it's all right," I mumbled.

"It's a stupid film, all that singing and spinning around on hills, it's a baby's movie."

"How do you know about the spinning around on hills? You must have seen it."

Awful Agatha snarled at me. She had bad breath and her teeth were definitely starting to turn yellow. Why didn't her parents tell her to brush her teeth every morning and every night?

"I've seen clips on YouTube, you silly *****," she said.

I refuse to write what she really called me, even in my private life story. But the rude word was certainly rude enough to send Miss Shufflebottom over.

"What's all the noise over there?" she asked.

She knew exactly what the noise was. It was coming from Awful Agatha's foul mouth as usual.

"There's nothing wrong with *The Sound of Music*," I said.

"Only if you're a moron," Awful Agatha shouted. "Singing and dancing stupid songs is for babies. Are you a baby, Sabrina? Do you cry when you watch it? I'm gonna tell the whole school that Sabrina thinks she's the pretty new girl, but really she sits in her bed and cries herself to sleep."

"Leave her alone!" said Charles. "She doesn't like watching

The Sound of Music! She likes dressing up in princess dresses!"

Charles stood up, puffed out his chest and smiled at me. He was one of the smallest, skinniest boys in class and much shorter than Awful Agatha.

He had a really big heart. He also had a really small brain.

He didn't understand the rules about grown-up girls. We don't dress up in babyish princess dresses at our age.

No wonder Awful Agatha had never looked happier.

"Sabrina likes to dress up as a princess?"

Miss Shufflebottom stepped between our two desks. "All right, girls, let's focus on our work now, please."

"Yes, Miss Shufflebottom, sorry," Awful Agatha said. "Oh, Miss Shufflebottom, I have a question?"

Miss Shufflebottom clearly didn't trust the bully. "Is it a serious question, Agatha?"

"Yes, of course, Miss Shufflebottom. It's a question about history."

"Ok," Miss Shufflebottom said, really slowly. "Go on then."

"In history, Miss, in the olden days, did other girls our age wear soppy princess dresses as well?"

The class roared with laughter. Every other student turned towards me. All I could see was their chattering teeth, all giggling at me like a pack of wild hyenas. Miss Shufflebottom raised her arms.

"That's enough, settle down, everyone. And no more questions from you, Agatha, I think you've said enough this morning."

"What's wrong, Miss? I'm only asking if princess dresses are for little babies or big babies like Sabrina."

"OH, JUST SHUT YOUR FACE, AGATHA."

I knew I was in serious trouble as soon as I'd finished the sentence. But I didn't care anymore. I hated the town, the school and everyone laughing at me.

Most of all, I hated *her*.

Awful Agatha leaned back on her chair until it bumped into my desk. She turned her head just enough so I could see half of her scowling face.

"When the bells goes," she whispered, "you're dead."

CHAPTER FOURTEEN

Charles followed me around the playground. He probably thought he was my bodyguard, even though he was a bit of a weed. I didn't need his help, but I was glad he was with me. I didn't feel like being alone.

My stomach was in a right mess. I couldn't stop thinking about Awful Agatha so I was in no mood for food. Besides, the menu was rubbish anyway. I knew the school canteen wasn't going to have the same choices as the Palace kitchen, but did we have to eat mac and cheese every day? I didn't even know what mac and cheese was at first. I kept hearing about this "Mac" and thought he was a greedy boy in school who ate loads of cheese. The Palace chef made macaroni with chicken and broccoli, which was green and fresh and yummy. But mac and cheese was yellow and looked like a canary's vomit.

So I watched Charles slurp down his mac and cheese and I started to relax a bit. Awful Agatha seemed to have vanished.

"Maybe she'll leave me alone," I said. "You've got cheese sauce on your chin."

Charles wiped his mouth on his blazer cuff. "Maybe she will," he said. "Maybe it's because I'm here protecting you."

Charles was a funny boy. "Yeah, maybe that's the reason," I replied, trying not to laugh.

The more I relaxed, the hungrier I started to get. Suddenly, my cold plate of mac and cheese didn't look so bad. "Maybe I could just have one spoonful of ... OW!"

The whole right side of my face started stinging. I heard girly voices giggling and suddenly felt wet. Water was dripping down my cheek and onto my school blazer. I looked up at the sky. It wasn't raining and we were sitting beneath the canteen's rusty old roof. Then I noticed something rubbery on my shoulder.

It was a water balloon!

That weasel-faced troll had smacked me in the face with a water balloon! Without thinking, I was on my feet. I had one leg in front of the other and my fists held up high, one protecting my chin and the other protecting my chest. This was my taekwondo-fighting stance. I spun around on my back heel and there she was, Awful Agatha. We were face-to-face.

"Ooh," she said. "It's the Karate Kid!"

Her dopey donkey friends laughed, but not as much as before. They didn't expect me to pull out my fantastic taekwondo-fighting stance. To be honest, I didn't expect me to, either. Uncle Ernie would not be amused. In fact, I could hear his voice rattling around my brain.

Remember, taekwondo makes you a strong, confident young woman. Taekwondo is not for attacking people. Princesses do not attack people.

But princesses do not get bullied in the school playground either. I was so confused. I knew that I should step away.

But I also wanted to kick Awful Agatha's backside until it was redder than a baboon's bottom.

Even she was shocked. She didn't seem quite as tough now that she was facing my invincible taekwondo-fighting stance. Charles looked shocked, too, but he always seemed shocked, so that didn't really count.

I took one teeny-tiny step backwards. "I don't want to fight," I said calmly.

"Yeah? Then why are you waving your fists at me?" she shouted.

"You threw a water balloon at my face."

"You don't know it was me. You're a lying pig!"

"I do know it was you. You throw water at other people because you don't need it. You never wash your face!"

I didn't sound like a princess anymore, but no one had called me a "lying pig" before. Awful Agatha's face changed colour. She looked like a squishy plum now.

"I'm gonna smash your face in!" she screamed.

She swung a punch at me. She actually swung a punch at me.

But it was nothing like one of Uncle Ernie's punches. It was slow and messy and really easy to avoid. I turned my shoulder and her fist sailed past me. Awful Agatha lost her balance and slipped.

Charles and one or two of the other girls giggled, but they soon stopped when Awful Agatha jumped back to her feet.

"Don't you dare laugh at me," she roared. "No one is ever allowed to laugh at me, not in my school. When I've sorted her out, I'm coming after you."

She pointed a finger between Charles' eyes. I thought he was going to burst into tears.

Then she kicked me!

She probably expected to catch me off guard, but it wasn't like one of Uncle Ernie's roundhouse kicks. Her kick was like a slow-motion TV replay of a goal. I had enough time to step aside. I flicked my arm to deflect her filthy shoe away from my blazer.

She looked like a spinning top, going around in circles. She couldn't stay on her feet and toppled over, slapping her legs against the concrete playground.

The laughter was definitely getting louder now.

"Agatha, let's stop now," I said softly.

She brushed the dirt and grit away from her muddy knees. "No! I don't get hit at school, ok? Nobody ever hits me at school, not here, never!"

"But I haven't hit you, Agatha."

"Yeah, well, I'm gonna hit you!"

And she charged at me.

She stretched her arms out wide like a huge washing line and raced towards me. Her green blazer flapped in the wind. She looked like a mad frog. Her sharp fingernails looked like eagle's claws. There wasn't time to go left or right. This time, she had me trapped. But then, in a split second, I remembered Uncle Ernie's shoelaces trick.

I dropped to the floor, as if I needed to tie my shoelaces in an emergency. Awful Agatha flew over my head and shoulders like a crazy Supergirl and kept flying until she knocked over a giant, grey bucket. But this wasn't any old giant, grey bucket. This was the giant, grey bucket where we scraped our canteen plates. It was full of leftover mac and cheese, strawberry yoghurt and rotting bananas. The mushed-up food scraps splattered everywhere and turned the floor into a slide.

Awful Agatha slid right through the lot.

No one was laughing now. At first, she didn't move. There were pasta pieces in her hair. She had black banana bits hanging from her earlobes like fruity earrings. She was face down in a puddle of strawberry yoghurt.

Charles grabbed my elbow. "Can a person drown in strawberry yoghurt?"

"Be quiet, Charles," I muttered.

I took a couple of careful steps towards her. The floor was so slippery. "Er, Agatha, are you ok? Come on, let me help you up."

I was about to lend a hand, when the crowd suddenly parted. Miss Shufflebottom and Miss Cannington pushed their way through the students.

"Come on, boys and girls, step aside," Miss Cannington ordered.

"I saw them fighting from the staffroom window," Miss Shufflebottom said.

"Yes, well, let's see what we can…oh my, Agatha, is that you?"

The two teachers looked truly horrified, totally speechless. Miss Shufflebottom crouched down beside Awful Agatha and gently turned her over.

"DON'T YOU TOUCH ME," she screamed. "NO ONE IS ALLOWED TO TOUCH ME! EVER!"

Now Miss Shufflebottom looked ready to burst into tears. Miss Cannington crossed her arms to show us all how cross she was. She was also careful not to get cheese sauce on her flat, open-toed sandals.

"Ok, Agatha, no one's going to touch you," the headmistress said. "You can get up in your own time and tell us how all this mess happened."

Finally, Awful Agatha rolled over. Everyone gasped. She looked like an alien. Her face was full of yellow and pink streaks and she was already covered in flies. She spat out some banana peel and wiped her mouth.

"I didn't make this mess," Agatha shouted. "She did!"

And she pointed straight at me.

CHAPTER FIFTEEN

Schools do stupid things. They make you sit next to the person that you've just had a fight with. No one else does that, do they? When two boxers have a punch-up, they don't have a chat in the office straight after, do they?

But that's what the old Cannibal did.

The headmistress made us sit at her neat desk in her neat office, while she adjusted her neat hair and glasses. She was quite pretty really, but she always tried to look as frumpy as possible. Miss Quick-Pants was the same at the Palace. She usually wore trousers, long-sleeved shirts and flat shoes and was never trendy. I asked my mother about it once and she said she envied Miss Quick-Pants' freedom. I was baffled: Who wants the freedom to dress like a zombie?

But maybe it's a teacher's thing. The old Cannibal had the same boring, predictable dress sense. She had the straight, brown trousers, the long-sleeved white shirt and flat sandals that those bearded men wear when they play guitar outside train stations. She stirred her tea and stared at us. Her silver spoon kept tapping against the side of the cup. It was seriously getting on my nerves, but at least it stopped me thinking about Awful Agatha.

She stank. And I mean really, really stank, worse than mouldy fish. We sat side by side and I tried not to look at her. I really tried. The old Cannibal had offered Awful Agatha some napkins to clean her face, but the idiot just screamed and threw them on the ground. She still had pinkish, reddish strawberry stripes and orangey, yellowish pasta stripes running down her face. But she wouldn't clean herself. She just sat there, shaking and clenching her fists.

But her clothes really ponged. The old Cannibal had already explained that all the food scraps, which she called slop, were thrown in that giant, grey bucket and sent to the farm. The farmers collected all the canteen leftovers from all the schools in the town and shovelled the lot into huge troughs to feed their pigs. This was pigswill, the smelly bits of food that no other human being would ever want to eat. And Awful Agatha was covered in the stuff.

I tried not to take a deep breath. I was seriously worried that I might throw up, but smells are strange. They pull your nose towards them like a magnet, even the horrible ones. Back at the Palace, my royal cousins would blow off at bedtime and then pull the silk sheets over their heads to smell themselves. They would pop their heads out to tell me that it was worse than a stink bomb. Then they'd dive under the sheets and smell themselves again!

Awful Agatha was like that. Her odour dragged my nostrils towards her. I turned, sniffed the air and must have pulled a face.

"I am going to kill you," she hissed. "I am going to grab your long, dumb hair and I'm going to ..."

"No one is going to grab anything. No one is going to kill anyone," sighed Miss Cannington.

I had almost forgotten about the old Cannibal stirring her tea with her noisy silver spoon. The rotten smell of pigswill had scrubbed my memory.

"I am, Miss. I'm going to drown her in the pig's bucket and I don't care what happens to me after that," Awful Agatha declared.

I couldn't believe what I was hearing. At the Palace, I got into trouble for going to the toilet without asking permission. I would never dream of telling Miss Quick-Pants that I was going to drown one of my royal cousins in a pig's dinner. I was waiting for Miss Cannington to go nuts, but she just smiled instead. She really was a weird headmistress.

"There's no need to perform now, Agatha," she said. "There's nobody here but me and Sabrina. You really should save the drama for the school play."

"I don't wanna be in your stupid school play."

Miss Cannington frowned. "I know you don't, Agatha. You never want to do anything, do you?"

Awful Agatha leered at me. "There's one thing that I definitely want to do."

Miss Cannington tapped the side of her cup with her spoon. "Ok, that's enough. There is clearly an issue between the two of you and I intend to get to the bottom of it. Why were you fighting outside?"

Awful Agatha crossed her arms and grinned. So the old Cannibal looked at me.

"Well, I wasn't, you know, like, fighting, Miss," I stammered.

"Miss Cannington."

"Sorry, I wasn't fighting, Miss Cannington."

"No, you were fighting with Agatha. And I must tell you, Sabrina, I am most disappointed. This school has a strict policy when it comes to physical assault. You cannot put your hands on another student."

"But I didn't," I cried. "I really didn't."

The old Cannibal raised an eyebrow. She was doing that teacher thing that is supposed to show how smart she is and how dumb she thinks I am for making up such a ridiculous story.

"I'm telling the truth, Miss Cannington. I did not touch her!"

The headmistress' eyes moved from side to side, like a pair of pinballs. I knew what she was thinking. I was the new girl in school picking a fight with the meanest bully in the school. I wanted to be the new No.1, the toughest girl in school. And look at me: no cuts, no bruises, not even a scratch. My vomit-coloured green blazer was still a vomit-coloured green blazer. It wasn't torn or dirty. My face wasn't muddy or bleeding.

But the biggest, angriest girl in the whole school was filthy. She was covered in pasta shapes and squishy chunks of bananas. Her knees, hands and elbows were red, scratched and puffy from falling into the pigswill. She looked like the bullied. I looked like the bully.

I knew the real truth about my taekwondo lessons with Uncle Ernie, but I couldn't tell that truth. And Awful Agatha knew the real truth about looking a total idiot in the playground, but she couldn't tell that truth either.

So we sulked and sat in silence.

"It looks like you are both leaving me with no choice,"

Miss Cannington said. "The school may have to consider suspension. Sabrina, I will speak to your guardian and explain to him that this is a final warning. Any more fighting and you will be suspended. Agatha, you've had more final warnings than I care to remember. None of them have worked. So, you're suspended."

Awful Agatha suddenly changed. I mean, really changed, in a second. She stopped slouching and sat up straight. Her eyes were all wide and watery. For the first time, she didn't look so awful. She looked average, normal. In fact, she seemed to shrink, as if she was turning into a little girl.

She looked scared.

"What does suspension mean?" she asked.

"You know what suspension means, Agatha. You will not be allowed to come to school for one week. You need to seriously take some time to think about your actions. It will also go on your record. I suspect you won't particularly care now, but it'll matter later, if you're applying for colleges or jobs."

Miss Cannington picked up the phone on her desk.

"Ok, I'll behave, Miss. Sorry."

Awful Agatha blurted out the words. Just like that. It was amazing.

"You've said that before, Agatha, and yet here we are."

"No, I will, Miss Cannington. I promise. I will stop fighting and work harder in class."

Miss Cannington held the phone in the air. "This isn't your first fight, Agatha, and I suspect it won't be your last. You won't even tell me what happened to cause this one."

"It was me, Miss Cannington. It was all me."

The headmistress raised her eyebrow again. "What was all you?"

"The fight in the canteen. I started it. I threw a water balloon at her and then I attacked her."

Miss Cannington pointed at Awful Agatha's ruined clothes. "Then how did you—?"

"I fell over," she interrupted, looking down at the floor. "I tried to punch her, but she moved out of the way. I tried to kick her, but she moved out of the way and I lost my balance. And then I dived on her, but she ... you know ..."

"Moved out of the way?"

"Yes. She moved out of the way and I slipped and fell into the bucket."

"Sabrina never attacked you?"

"No."

"You got all those cuts and scrapes without Sabrina actually touching you?"

"Yeah. And don't tell anyone either. But that's what happened, all right? So you can't suspend me now because we never actually had a fight and I told you the truth. Right?"

Miss Cannington tapped her fingers on the desk. "Is this true, Sabrina?"

"Yes, Miss Cannington."

"Are you agreeing with Agatha because you think it will get you out of trouble?"

"No, Miss Cannington."

"Are you, like, a karate expert or something?"

"No, Miss Cannington."

That one actually wasn't really a little white lie. I'm not a karate expert. I'm an epic taekwondo expert.

The old Cannibal continued with her finger tapping on the desk. "I'm not sure what to say."

"Say you won't suspend me, Miss," Awful Agatha mumbled.

"You still threw punches and kicks. You said so yourself and this is your second incident with Sabrina in a week."

"Ok, I'll leave her alone. I promise not to bother her any more, in class, in the playground, everywhere, all right? Is that enough?"

Miss Cannington decided to look at me. "Do you agree to do the same?"

"Yes, Miss Cannington."

She hummed to herself for ages. "Hmm, ok, I'll put a suspension on hold, Agatha, on the condition that you stay away from Sabrina. That means no more fighting, no more arguing and no more irritating each other. Agreed?"

We both nodded. Miss Cannington started dialling her phone.

"Wait, what are you doing, Miss?" Awful Agatha said. "You said no suspensions."

"I know what I said, Agatha, but I still want to have a chat with both your parents. I believe in clear communication channels between parents and teachers at our school."

She held the phone to her ear. "I'm going to speak to your guardian first, Sabrina."

CHAPTER SIXTEEN

We didn't talk to each other in the van. I was being a bit childish, but that's because I *am* a child. What was Uncle Ernie's excuse? He just peered through the windscreen as the wipers swished back and forth.

Normally, I love the rain. We used to get these terrifying storms back at the Palace. Mummy squeezed me whenever the thunder exploded over the Palace. Daddy always laughed and handed me a cup of hot chocolate and some marshmallows.

He always said the same thing: *Only two marshmallows for you, Sabrina, you're already sweet enough.*

And then, he'd plop a third marshmallow into my hot chocolate when Mummy wasn't looking. It was our little secret. He'd wink at me and I'd wink back. That was the secret signal of our Three Marshmallows Club.

I kept thinking about them in Uncle Ernie's filthy white van. I blamed the rubbish weather. The rain splattered across the windscreen, which made me think of my Palace bedroom, and mugs of hot chocolate and Mummy's hugs and Daddy's extra marshmallows.

But I knew deep down that it wasn't just the weather. It was everything.

"So you're not going to say anything, then?" Uncle Ernie asked.

He was obviously disappointed in me. It was easy to tell when Uncle Ernie was upset because he never ever said that he was upset. He just sat in silence. I don't know if it was a cunning plan or not, but the silence often made me feel worse.

"I've got nothing to say," I grunted.

If he was going to sulk, then I was going to sulk. I watched his hands grip the steering wheel. His knuckles were turning white so he was obviously squeezing too hard.

"I've got nothing to say either," he said, which probably meant he had loads of things to say.

"Good!" I cried.

"Yeah, good!" he replied.

I folded my arms in a huff. Uncle Ernie focused on driving through the storm.

"I can't believe you used taekwondo in school," he muttered to himself, but I still heard him.

"I didn't use taekwondo," I said.

"Please, Sabrina. I know we have to use little white lies out there, but not in here, not with each other. We've always got to be honest with each other."

"I am being honest! That horrible girl threw a punch at me, then she tried to kick me and then she charged at me like a mad bull. What was I supposed to do? Let her attack me?"

Uncle Ernie cleared his throat. "Yeah, maybe."

This time, my eyes didn't sting. My cheeks did. They were on fire. I felt a scary rage shoot all the way through my body, up from my toes to my cheeks. I was much angrier now than I ever was with Awful Agatha.

"You *wanted* me to get hurt?"

I wiped my face as fast as I could, but I'm sure that Uncle Ernie had already seen the tears.

"No, of course not, that's the last thing I'd want."

Uncle Ernie's voice sounded wobbly and funny. He was probably upset, too, but I didn't really care. That's what happens when you say mean things to people. I wasn't going to let him off the hook, not this time.

"So you *didn't* want me to get hurt, but you wanted her to attack me?"

"That's not what I said, Sabrina," he replied.

"Yes, you did."

"No, I said maybe you had to let her attack you. Children fight in the playground. Sometimes, they win. Sometimes, they lose. That's life."

He wasn't making any sense at all. In fact, he was seriously getting on my nerves.

"But you're always telling me that taekwondo is for defence," I said. "So I defended myself."

Uncle Ernie slammed on the brakes. The seatbelt tugged against my shoulder. The rusty white van swerved across the road and splashed through a puddle. We stopped beside the kerb. Uncle Ernie closed his eyes and took a really deep breath. I thought he was praying.

"Sabrina, I have been teaching you taekwondo since you were four years old because you are a princess. Most four year old girls do not learn taekwondo because most four year old girls are not princesses. Do you understand?"

"Not really."

"When the whole school sees you flipping the biggest bully into doggy poop, it's going to look suspicious, isn't it?"

"It was pigswill, actually. I wish it *was* doggy poop. I wish I had rubbed her nose in the doggy poop. In fact—"

"Yes, yes, I think that's enough doggy poop."

"It was pigswill!"

"Whatever. Just listen. Every kid in the school will be watching you from now on. And this headmistress of yours wants to speak to your mother and father, which we both know is impossible. I'll have to fix that."

"Good. Can you get one of our royal bodyguards to squash her?"

Uncle Ernie was in no mood for jokes, but neither was I. I wasn't joking. I wanted to squash them all into slime, turn them into pigswill and feed them to the hogs on the Palace farm.

"Sabrina, you really need to grow up. You have a responsibility to do the right thing now, not only for yourself, but for your parents."

Seriously? I mean, *seriously*? That was the last straw.

Miss Shufflebottom and the old Cannibal didn't really know me so I had to put up with their nonsense. Charles was a bit daft and Awful Agatha was like an ugly stepsister in one of those lame fairy tales. So I had to accept their stupidity and put up with their moronic comments. They didn't know my situation. But Uncle Ernie knew everything and even he was picking on me, accusing me of doing the wrong thing.

"I AM DOING THE RIGHT THING!" I shouted.

I really did shout, too. My eyes had turned into those garden sprinklers. But this was different. This was angry crying. The more I cried, the angrier I got, which was confusing. And the more confused I got, the more I cried, which made me even angrier. Basically, I was an angry, confused, leaking mess.

My soaking wet face and my sudden screaming had obviously scared Uncle Ernie because his expression changed. He looked all sweaty and nervous.

"Sabrina, why are you shouting?"

"I don't know why I'm shouting," I sobbed. "I don't know why I'm crying so much. I don't know anything anymore."

"Hey, it'll be all right."

Uncle Ernie took his seatbelt off and leaned over, but I brushed him away and stared out of the window. It was still pouring buckets.

"It won't be all right! My life is rubbish and you helped to make it rubbish by bringing me here. I didn't want to be here, did I? But you made me come here and then you tell me off for not doing the right thing. That's just mean and selfish. I don't want to be here. Everyone hates me here. I want to go home. I want people to like me again. I want to see my friends, my family and even Miss Quick-Pants. But most of all, I want to see my Mum and Dad. But I can't. Have you got any idea what that feels like? No, of course you don't. And then, and then, the only person I've got left in the whole world is you and now you're telling me off and shouting at me and ... that's ... really ... unfair!"

I was sobbing so much that my voice kept going up and down. Miss Quick-Pants once said that about 70 per cent of my body was filled with water. I reckon my water level must have dropped to 20 per cent while in the white van. My eyes had turned into hosepipes.

Uncle Ernie pulled out a handkerchief. "Here, wipe your eyes, Sabrina," he said quietly.

"I don't want your stupid hankie," I sobbed. "I want my parents."

"I know you do. Maybe one day—"

"No, not one day," I interrupted. "Tonight. I want to see my parents tonight."

Uncle Ernie didn't speak. He just nodded his head and started the engine. In fact, neither of us spoke for the rest of the journey. We just listened to the raindrops.

I'll never tell anyone this, but I wept all the way home.

CHAPTER SEVENTEEN

Uncle Ernie obviously felt guilty because he was up to something. When we got home, he ordered pizza. Actually, he ordered two cheese pizzas, without even asking first. Normally, I have to do my homework first or nag him for an hour to get a cheese pizza. But today I didn't have to do anything.

Then he started whistling. He always whistled when he was working and he was making a right racket in the room next door. That was Uncle Ernie's room. He called it his "shed", but really it was just a dining room with a table full of laptops, cables, modems, scanners and printers.

He told me I was not to enter the room without his permission. He would call me when he was ready. Whenever he popped into the living room to check on me, he smiled and clapped his hands together. He always did this when he was excited. But I'm not stupid. I knew this was his way of not talking about our argument in the van. Uncle Ernie didn't like arguments, not with me anyway. He preferred them with grown-ups. In fact, he really liked arguments with older, tougher guys.

At the Palace, everyone had a story about Uncle Ernie. The cooks, the housemaids, the gardeners, everybody gossiped about him.

There was the one about my father and a man in the crowd who wouldn't let go of his hand, so Uncle Ernie karate-chopped the man's arm until it fell off.

Then there was the time my mother was walking in the Palace gardens and a python slithered towards her, so Uncle Ernie tied the snake into a knot and threw it into the lake.

And then, there was a burglar who tried to break into the Palace and Uncle Ernie jumped through his bedroom window on the third floor, flew through the air and landed on the burglar's back.

I didn't believe any of the stories. I wasn't gullible like the other kids. Uncle Ernie wasn't some movie superhero. He was just my Uncle Ernie.

But he was fearless. That was definitely true. Nothing scared him, ever. In fact, I think there's only one creature on this planet that just might terrify him.

Me.

Whenever we have an argument, he always gives up first. And after that, he always tries to cheer me up, which is when he does all that smiling and clapping and ordering pizzas.

I think I know why he behaves in this way. It's the same reason why I can never stay angry with him for too long. Even when he makes me so mad I think my head is going to explode and spray blood and skull all over my bedroom wall. But I soon calm down. So does Uncle Ernie. He's scared of upsetting me because he, well, you know. Well, I know why and Uncle Ernie knows why and that's all that matters. I don't want my story to sound like a soppy fairy tale.

"Ok, I'm ready," Uncle Ernie's voice called out from the dining room. "Are you excited?"

"Yes, Uncle Ernie, I'm *totally* excited," I lied.

I didn't want to hurt his feelings. I already knew he had pizza waiting for me. I'd overheard him ordering on the phone. But I knew how to look surprised to see pizzas on the table.

I opened the dining room door. There were no pizzas. In fact, there was nothing special in the room ... except ... except ... it was hard to explain. I suddenly felt woozy. The room whizzed around me. Even Uncle Ernie was blurred. He was pointing at something weird. Were they aliens? Monsters? Whatever they were, they were making my brain spin.

"Say hello to your Mum and Dad."

Uncle Ernie was talking gibberish again. Even at the Palace, he loved to talk gobbledygook to make the other kids laugh. But this wasn't particularly funny at all. This was cruel.

Maybe I was dreaming. That's what it was. I once read a book about witches' spells and potions and it said that if you were ever under a spell that made you fall asleep, pinch yourself to check if you're awake or dreaming.

So I pinched myself.

"Ow," I said.

"What's wrong?" Uncle Ernie asked.

"I pinched myself to check if I'm dreaming."

Uncle Ernie grinned at me. "Oh, you are definitely awake. Come and see."

He held my hand and pulled me towards the blurry creatures. I rubbed my eyes.

"Hello, Sabrina," said the Man Alien.

"Oh, Sabrina," said the Woman Alien. And then she burst into tears.

And then I burst into tears, which was a bit embarrassing. I'd watched loads of movies about aliens before and they'd never made me cry.

The room was still swirling and my legs felt tingly. Uncle Ernie plonked me on a chair in front of the aliens.

"Take a deep breath," he whispered. "You seem like you're in shock."

I took his advice. With every breath, the spinning room slowed down. My eyesight was getting better, too. The aliens were disappearing and turning into ... my parents! They were waving at me from one of Uncle Ernie's laptops! Daddy was smiling. Mummy was crying. And then I realised that I was still crying and smiling and waving.

"Ok, Sabrina, I've had to use a VPN, a cloaking device and all kinds of hacking tools to make sure this Skype call is untraceable," Uncle Ernie said quickly. "So, to be on the safe side, I think you can have five minutes to talk to your parents."

I had no idea what my EPIC, AWESOME and WONDERFUL Uncle Ernie was going on about. But I knew I wasn't going to waste a single second.

CHAPTER EIGHTEEN

Mummy and Daddy were sitting in the Palace dining room. I could see the framed paintings of all our relatives on the wall behind them. They were both wearing their fancy, frilly clothes that Daddy secretly hated, so they must have just finished a royal engagement. That's probably why they kept waving at me. They wave all day. Whenever they see someone, they just start waving without thinking. Even when it's me.

I had so many things to say. I didn't know where to start. So I wiped my eyes and decided to say the only thing that mattered to me. I had to get it off my chest, right at the start.

"When can I come home?" I blurted out.

I realised I'd made a bit of a mistake straightaway. Mummy's waterworks started again. Daddy kept touching his eyes with a handkerchief. I told myself that he was probably suffering from hay fever.

"Ah, it's good to hear your voice, dear," Daddy said.

Normally, I can't stand it when he calls me a "dear" because I don't have four legs and antlers, but today I didn't mind at all. I was happy for him to call me "dear" forever.

"Things are a little complicated at the moment," Daddy continued.

"Are the people still not happy with us? That's crazy.

We're such a cool Royal Family. Mummy looks pretty in all her frilly dresses and Daddy shakes so many hands."

The Skype picture was not great. The picture kept freezing, which turned my parents into royal waxworks. But I still saw Daddy laugh.

"Yes, I do shake a lot of hands, Sabrina," he said. "But for some people, that's not enough anymore. They think I should do more for their taxes."

"But we don't use their taxis. We have limos."

Mummy smiled and whispered something to Daddy about not discussing politics with me. That was fine by me. Daddy wasn't making any sense anyway.

"How is your new school?" Mummy asked.

Uncle Ernie leaned over and held my hand. "We're getting there," he said. "Isn't that right, Sabrina?"

I shrugged my shoulders. "It's all right. An old cannibal runs the school. My teacher has the stupidest name ever for a teacher. She's called Miss Shufflebottom."

Daddy thought that was hilarious. His giggling made me giggle.

"I know, right? Miss Shufflebottom. That's her real name. She's probably not as smart as Miss Quick-Pants either."

My mother frowned.

"Sorry, I mean Miss Cruickshanks. But she might be kinder and softer. She's just a bit wet when it comes to dealing with girls like Awful Agatha."

My parents looked at each other.

"And who's Awful Agatha?" Daddy asked.

"Well, she's just Agatha really, but I call her Awful Agatha because she's totally awful and cruel and she smells, too, like a really bad smell, like that smell in the pony stables. But it's not just the smell. She doesn't like me. Actually, I reckon she hates me. And I can't stand her either. I know you say I shouldn't hate anyone. Princesses don't hate anyone. I do try, but I can't help it. She's vile and smelly and I can't stand her. But we've agreed to leave each other alone for now."

Uncle Ernie's elbow nudged me under the table. "But you've got Charlie," he said.

"Ooh, who's Charlie," Daddy said. "Is he your boyfriend? Can she marry a boy called Charlie? What do you think, Beverly? Everybody stand for Prince Charlie of the House of Valence! I'm not sure if the name has a royal ring to it."

I must have been blushing because Mummy told Daddy to stop teasing me about Charles. Normally, I would've agreed with her but not this time. I wanted Daddy to make fun of me all day and all night.

"Just ignore your father, Sabrina," Mummy said. "Charlie sounds like a lovely boy. I'm pleased you're making friends. We know this hasn't been easy for you and Uncle Ernie has told us what happened at school."

I gave Uncle Ernie my angry eyes. I had no idea he'd already told them about my playground fight with Awful Agatha and the pigswill.

"It's all right, you're not in trouble," Mummy said, obviously seeing my worried face. "But the school wants to speak to us and Uncle Ernie says they are being very persistent. This is very difficult for all of us. Uncle Ernie may try to organise a private phone call in the next few days. But we all need to try really hard to keep a low profile and stay safe."

"I know, Mummy. It's just ... I miss you both so much."

"Oh, we miss you too, so much, every single day."

My throat started to throb, but I was determined not to cry again. I needed this Skype call to be a happy memory so I could remember it every night at bedtime. Luckily, I had a silly idea.

"Daddy, tell me about Mr Cotton, the Palace gardener, again. Please!"

Daddy held Mummy's hand and smiled. "Ok, very quickly. When you were five years old, you liked to throw sticks for the puppies to fetch in the Palace gardens. One day, you threw a stick too high and it landed in an oak tree that grew over the lake. You were insistent that you didn't want another stick. So you called over Mr Cotton. He was an old-fashioned, traditional man and very, very skinny. He held up his ugly, green trousers with a rope. And you asked him to reach up into the tree for your stick. He complained and grumbled, as he always did, but agreed to help you. As he stretched his long body, the rope came loose and his trousers fell down. Now Mr Cotton was a stubborn old man who didn't believe in wearing underwear. So he flashed his backside at everyone in the Palace gardens, including you. Then you screamed, which made him jump. He lost his balance and fell into the lake. I have never seen anyone swim so fast in my entire life. His bare bottom cut through the water like a shark's fin. He was terrified that the ducks would bite his bum."

We all laughed about Mr Cotton's backside. I knew that we'd all heard the story hundreds of times before, but we kept laughing. None of us wanted to stop laughing, not even Uncle Ernie.

That's why I didn't hear the tapping at first. I was too busy laughing. Then the tapping got louder so I laughed louder. I didn't want that miserable storm to spoil my chat with my parents. The raindrops could tap away at the windows. Nothing was going to stop me spending time with my family.

And then I saw him.

Charles was outside, banging on the dining room window and waving at us. He could see Uncle Ernie fiddling with his cables. Worst of all, he could see me talking to a laptop, talking to King Halbutt and Queen Beverly of the House of Valence.

Uncle Ernie leapt across the table and slammed the laptop shut.

I didn't even get a chance to say goodbye.

CHAPTER NINETEEN

Charles is a funny boy. He doesn't have many friends and it's easy to see why. For a start, he's weird. He spends all his spare time solving detective maths puzzles. He's rubbish at all sports, especially football, and doesn't read comics or watch action movies. He's the complete opposite of all the boys back at the Palace. The princes and dukes were all strong and sporty and full of muscles. They rode horses, played polo, did fencing and martial arts and were always fighting each other. They were also always showing off, which got really dull after a while.

In the Palace gardens, they shouted the same things at me. *Sabrina, come and see me play polo ... Sabrina, come and watch my fencing lessons ... Sabrina, look at my huge, bulging biceps.* They thought they were the coolest boys ever. I thought they were the most annoying boys ever. They wore the same, silly clothes and looked and sounded like royal robots.

That's why I like Charles. I don't want to hang around with a tall, handsome, athletic prince. I want to hang out with Charles. He's small and shy and a little bit soft. He's like a little brother who needs protecting. I don't have any brothers or sisters so I'm stuck with Charles. I don't have any other friends either. Charles is my only friend and maybe my best friend, too.

But sometimes, I really want to kick Charles in the privates.

He's too nosey! He's like a spy who wants to know everything. Or a tiny piece of mud stuck to my shoe. I can't get rid of him.

I had to drag him down the street to get him away from the house. At first, I was furious with him. He had taken me away from my parents. I seriously thought about kicking him where it would hurt most. In our self-defence class, Uncle Ernie taught me a low round kick that's perfect for whacking naughty boys in the privates. But I didn't. Charles can't really defend himself and taekwondo is only for self-defence, not for attacking children who can't fight back. Anyway, I'm pretty sure that princesses are not supposed to kick anyone in the privates.

I stopped Charles at a small playground at the end of the street. There was a slide, a roundabout and some rusty swings. I gently shoved him onto one of the swings. Well, I thought it was a gentle shove.

"Ow, that hurt," Charles whimpered, rubbing his arm.

"Don't be such a wimp," I replied in a huff.

I sat on the swing beside him. He was still rubbing his arm, which made me feel a little sorry for him. He had these big, brown eyes that made him look like one of the puppies at the Palace. My anger began to slip away. I didn't want to boot him between the legs anymore.

But I was still fed up with him.

"Why do you keep following me?" I asked.

Charles blinked a few times. That's all I needed: more tears after a day of non-stop blubbing.

"I wasn't following you," he said in a tiny voice.

He rocked back and forth on the swing, staring at his scuffed school shoes.

"If you weren't following me, why were you in my garden then? Are you a garden gnome? You look like a garden gnome."

Charles straightened his spectacles. "No, I'm not a garden gnome and don't make fun of my height!"

"I'm not making fun of your height. I'm making fun of you. Gnomes hang around people's gardens. That's you! I want to know why you were spying on me again. I open my front door. You're there. I look out of my window. You're there. You're like a stalker."

Charles seemed puzzled. "What's a stalker?"

"You. You're a stalker, someone who keeps following someone else."

"I'm not! I just wanted to see if you were ok after the fight with Agatha. I'm not a stormtrooper."

"Stalker! It's a stalker. And I'm fine!"

"Then why are you shouting at me?"

"Because you stopped me from talking to my ... I mean, on my laptop. I couldn't ... oh, it doesn't matter. I'm fine now!"

"You don't sound fine. Do you think Agatha will keep bullying you?"

"*Awful.* Her name is *Awful* Agatha. No, she can't. She'll get suspended if she comes near me again."

"Good. I really don't like her," Charles mumbled.

"Yeah, well, I really hate her."

We sat in silence for a while. Then Charles bumped his swing against my swing. So I bumped my swing against his swing. We giggled a bit. Charles should laugh more often. He looks less weedy when he laughs.

He stopped bumping me and wiped his spectacles. He was sweating and they had steamed up. He put them back on and squinted at me.

"Sabrina, can I ask you something?"

"No, Charles, you do not look like a garden gnome."

"No, not that. Something else. Who were you talking to on the laptop?"

My throat felt ticklish. I found it hard to swallow. "What are you going on about?"

"On those laptops. Were you making a video or something?"

I felt a surge of relief hit my body like a bolt of lightning. "Yeah, I was making a video."

Charles kicked a clump of soggy mud under the swing. He didn't want to look at me. "I don't think you were," he said, really softly.

"You don't know what I was doing. You were outside, spying."

"I think I do. I'm like a detective."

"You're like an idiot."

"I solve detective puzzles every day. I do maths and English puzzles. Remember?"

"Er, not really."

Of course I remembered. I remembered everything. But I wanted to change the subject. I didn't want Charles to be a detective. That was dangerous. I wanted Charles the Weedy Boy Who Was Rubbish At Sports to come back. That was much better. Even Charles the Garden Gnome was better than Charles the Detective Busybody. He could get me in a whole lot of trouble.

"Yeah, well, I know how to be a detective," he said. "You look at all the evidence. You pick the best evidence and examine it and then you reach a conclusion."

"You're nuts," I said.

But I was the one going nuts. I had to sit on my hands to hide them. They were shaking too much.

"No, I've put it altogether. First, you arrive out of nowhere, but you seem really smart and confident, compared to the other girls."

I shrugged my shoulders. "I went to a good school before, better than this dump."

But Charles the Detective Busybody ignored me.

"Then you are shy to talk about where you come from or what you do at home. Then I come to your house and ..."

"You spied on my house!"

He rolled his eyes. "Then I came to your house and saw that strange photo of you, dressed up in fancy, expensive clothes."

"I told you, it was a photo from a theme park."

"Then you can fight the biggest girl in the school using taekwondo. No one at our school can fight like that. And no girl our age can fight like that. But you fight like Wonder Woman."

"No, Charles ..."

"And then, your uncle has all those computers. Why would anyone need three computers in one room? And you were sitting in front of them all, talking to people."

"I was only sitting in front of one of them."

"And that's when I worked it out all by myself. That's when I realised who you really are."

I felt the sweat running through my hair. My disgusting, green blazer was soaked. I couldn't see properly. My mouth felt dry, but I tried to speak. I had to know.

"Ok, Mr Clever Clogs," I croaked. "Who am I?"

Charles looked ever so pleased with himself.

"You're not just Sabrina Parslowe," he said. "You're a famous YouTube star!"

CHAPTER TWENTY

Being a fake YouTube star had some brilliant advantages. First, dopey Charles was no longer Charles the Detective Busybody. He was Charles the Soppy Fan.

He kept winking at me.

If I saw him in the school canteen, he winked at me. If I walked into the classroom, he winked at me. And if we were with other students in the playground, he tapped his nose. That was Charles the Soppy Fan pretending to be Charles the Cool Fan. He thought we were part of this celebrity secret. I was the celebrity and he was keeping the secret.

But his daft theory actually did me a massive favour. According to Charles, my strange, puzzling life had a simple explanation now. He could answer all the weird questions about me. Why do I not like to talk about my old life? Easy. I'm a YouTube star. I can't tell my millions of subscribers where I live, can I? Why do I have family photos where I'm dressed up like a princess? Well, that's obvious. I'm a YouTube star. I must have loads of fancy photo shoots, right? Why can't he find me on YouTube? My site is switched to private to protect my privacy. *Duh*!

YouTube stars always know life hacks and have awesome skills, like taekwondo. YouTube stars are always on their laptops. And YouTube stars must employ a hundred people to make their videos. I have Uncle Ernie. But he's worth more than a hundred people.

I was worried at first that Charles would get carried away with his YouTube-star theory. But it became our shared secret. He'd never had a shared secret with a friend before. He'd never really had many friends before. Now he had a friend who was a YouTube star. No way was he going to mess that up.

So he started acting like my celebrity agent.

One day, Miss Shufflebottom was teaching us geography. We were learning about the differences between towns, cities and countries. She went around the class asking each of us to stand up and say where we were born. Most of the students were all born in the same town. *This* town. It was a boring answer for a boring place.

And then she turned to me! I couldn't tell the truth, obviously. But I couldn't remember any of Uncle Ernie's little white lies either. He calls them cover stories. He says that spies all have cover stories and he loves making them up. It's just impossible to remember them all.

Miss Shufflebottom told me to stand up in front of the class.

"It's ok, Sabrina," she said. "You can tell us where you are from?"

"Erm, well, ok ... I think ..."

I stuttered. I coughed. I blushed. I fidgeted. I did everything except think of an answer that would send Miss Shufflebottom away.

Naturally, Awful Agatha loved every second of my humiliation. I could see the little witch giggling at me through the corner of my eye. I tried to think of her sliding through the pigswill, but it didn't help.

"You can tell us, Sabrina," Miss Shufflebottom said. "Every one in the class is going to participate so we will all have a turn. Where were you born?"

I was born in Mulakating, you wobbly old custard! When I was born, there were street parties held all over the country. I was born Princess Sabrina of the House of Valence, the only child of King Halbutt and Queen Beverly. I am part of a royal family that is having problems with the Government that I don't really understand. It's called politics. I call it a royal pain in the backside. If they weren't having these political problems, I'd still be a princess and you wouldn't be asking me all these dumb questions. Now take your bottom and shuffle off!

That's what I wanted to say anyway.

"Erm, I was born in ..."

"She doesn't like to say," Charles interrupted. "She's a bit shy, Miss Shufflebottom. And it makes her think of her parents, which makes her a bit sad."

Miss Shufflebottom nodded her head and hummed, like teachers do when they're pretending to be sympathetic. "Of course, I understand," she said.

She didn't.

When I sat down again, Charles winked at me. I wanted to flick him in his winking eye. Ok, that's a bit unfair. I didn't want to flick him, but I wasn't very pleased with him. He made me sound like a bit of a crybaby and I could already see Awful Agatha giggling.

But Charles *had* saved me. He thought he was protecting his YouTube Star, but the nincompoop had no idea that he was actually protecting an undercover princess.

To him, he was just looking after his friend.

And my life actually got a bit better. Ok, that's a HUGE exaggeration. My life was still miserable. I still missed my home and my parents and even Miss Quick-Pants. But my life wasn't getting any worse.

Awful Agatha really did stay away from me, at least most of the time. She whispered rude words when we passed each other in the classroom. She poked her tongue out at me in the canteen. And one time in the toilets, she walked in on me when I was washing my hands. She bent down and looked under all the toilet doors and realised we were alone. She gritted her teeth and walked towards me.

I thought she was going to crack me across the face. But she stopped, like she'd remembered something. Then she turned around and ran out of the toilets. I'll say one thing about her: She was terrified of being sent home from school. Once she got out of my hair, the other girls left me alone, too. Most girls are like that, aren't they? They hang around with the bullies only because they don't want to be bullied. As soon as Awful Agatha went away, they went away.

Charles and I were left alone in class and the canteen. I had time to think about my parents and the huge party they'd hold for me at the Palace when I returned. And he had time to ask me loads of ridiculous questions about being a YouTube star.

"Do you know any of the actors on the Disney Channel?" he asked me at lunchtime.

"No, Charles."

"What about CBeebies?"

"No, because I'm not five years old."

"You must know some of the celebrities on Nickelodeon, right?"

"Nickelodeon? Yeah, I know loads of actors on Nickelodeon."

"Wow! Really?"

"No."

Charles looked really disappointed as he slurped his chocolate milk. So I gave him a gentle elbow in the belly.

"But I know you," I said.

"Yeah, but I'm nobody."

"You're my friend."

We smiled at each other as the school bell rang. We were probably saved by the bell, too, as the smiling was getting a bit awkward.

Charles checked his watch. "It's not time to return to class."

Miss Shufflebottom arrived and sent us straight to the school hall. The place was packed. There were rows of children sitting with their legs crossed on the wooden floor. All those green blazers made the hall look like a giant puddle of sick.

Miss Shufflebottom put on her loud whisper voice and told us to sit down quickly. She was panicking a bit, which meant that Miss Cannington was on her way. Miss Shufflebottom always panicked when the old Cannibal was coming.

Our headmistress marched into the hall and stood in front of the entire school. She didn't speak at first. She just gazed at all the students. I'm surprised she didn't throw up. I couldn't stare at all those vomit-coloured blazers every day.

The Cannibal cleared her voice really loudly. That was the signal for all of us to shut up and stop fidgeting.

"Thank you for coming in so quickly and quietly," she said. "And I'm sorry to those of you who never had enough time to eat your lunches. Perhaps we can make some time after this assembly for you to finish. But I believe this is a serious matter that could not wait."

The Cannibal put her hands behind her back and stood up straight.

"This is an issue that needs to be settled right now," she said. "I'm not happy about it at all. But I believe that one of the students sitting here is a thief."

CHAPTER TWENTY-ONE

So now we had a criminal running around the classrooms. The Cannibal said he'd been doing it for months. He pinched wallets and purses, but was only interested in the money. The wallets and purses were dumped in the school bushes. The emergency school assembly was actually kind of fun. The gossip was fantastic!

As soon as the Cannibal said there was a thief sitting in the hall, everyone started looking over their shoulders, as if the thief was going to jump up and start waving. But we were all thinking and muttering the same stuff.

"Who do you think did it?" Charles mumbled.

"How would I know?" I shot back.

"Well, you're really clever."

"And you do all those detective quizzes. Who do *you* think it is?"

"I don't know."

"You're useless at being a detective."

At the front of the hall, the Cannibal did that loud coughing, throat-clearing thing. "Ahem, that'll do," she said. "This is a serious matter."

Of course it was a serious matter. For the rest of the day, we all talked about nothing else. Miss Shufflebottom said we must not speculate.

We all ignored her and speculated. Charles was certain it was some older boy in the next year called Liam. Charles didn't seem to have any evidence whatsoever, but Liam was a popular student who was really good at football and that seemed to bother Charles. I had no clue who the thief was and, to be honest, I wasn't particularly bothered either. I had bigger problems than someone stealing my lunch money, like maybe never seeing my parents again.

Miss Shufflebottom knew she had no chance of getting the class to concentrate, especially when she was trying to teach us equivalent fractions. Awful Agatha was getting super stressed. She kept making stupid comments about the maths questions, only because she was too thick to understand them.

When Miss Shufflebottom told her to imagine a cream cake cut into four quarters, the annoying brat said that she couldn't because Miss Shufflebottom would eat all four slices. That's why she had a shuffling bottom. Naturally, all the girls sitting around Awful Agatha laughed. But no one else really did. Her comments were really mean and dumb, but they still turned Miss Shufflebottom's cheeks into a couple of ripe tomatoes.

Luckily, most of the other kids were nattering away about the thief and not really paying attention. So Miss Shufflebottom did that teacher thing, where they take a bit of gossip and turn it into a classroom discussion. She wanted us to have a group debate on the importance of sharing instead. But that didn't make much sense to any of us. Even Charles got a bit frustrated.

"But why should you share your lunch money?" he said to the class when it was his turn to speak. "My parents work really hard for me. They give me lunch money so I can eat. It's mine. If someone takes it without permission, that's not sharing. It's stealing!"

Some of the other children in the class actually applauded Charles, which gave him a bit of a big head.

"They all clapped for me," he whispered.

"Yeah, some of them did," I pointed out.

"What was that, Sabrina?" Miss Shufflebottom said.

I glared at Charles' big head. "Look what you've done now," I hissed.

"Er, nothing, Miss Shufflebottom," I said in a much louder voice.

"Maybe you could share with us your thoughts on how your last school dealt with social issues like petty theft," Miss Shufflebottom said.

I stood up really slowly. "Well, we didn't really have any stealing at my last school."

"Yeah, 'cos she's a spoiled rich kid," Awful Agatha said loudly.

"Thank you, Agatha," Miss Shufflebottom said. "Remember the agreement we had?"

"Yeah, all right. Sorry, Miss."

"Not to me."

Miss Shufflebottom nodded in my direction.

Awful Agatha snarled at me. "Sorry, Sabrina," she said, not sorry at all.

"Thank you, Agatha," said Miss Shufflebottom. "Ok, Sabrina."

"Yeah, well, there wasn't really any stealing in my school because we had, er, very small classes. In fact, it was a very small school."

Miss Shufflebottom's eyes widened. "Ah, that's a very interesting discussion point, Sabrina. Is there perhaps a connection between the size of a community, in this case a school, and the number of crimes in a community?"

"I don't know, Miss Shufflebottom."

"Well, let's explore this topic further. How many students did you have, roughly?"

"About eight or nine."

Awful Agatha and her pack of hairy hyenas started giggling.

"Settle down, everyone," Miss Shufflebottom. "No, I didn't mean how many students in your class. I meant, how many students did you have in your school?"

"About eight or nine, Miss Shufflebottom."

Everyone was laughing now. Even Charles rolled his eyes. I realised straightaway that I'd made a big mistake. Obviously, regular schools had more students and bigger classes. Uncle Ernie had probably given me a little white lie for my fake school. But I had so many little white lies to remember I thought my brain was going to explode. Once, the Palace chef let me try and make some scrambled eggs in the microwave. But I left the eggs in there for too long and they splattered across the walls of the microwave. That's what my brain feels like most days.

"That's quite a small school, Sabrina, if there are *really* only eight or nine students. No wonder there wasn't any stealing," Miss Shufflebottom said. "What was the name of your school?"

My mind went blank. I knew I had an answer for this question, but the giggling had put me off. I couldn't even remember my own name, let alone a made-up name for my fake school in my fake town in my fake life.

"My last school? My last school was called ... Its name was ..."

I heard Awful Agatha laughing. What was so funny?

"Oh yes, that's it, the name of my last school was ..."

A bang on the classroom door made everyone jump. Even Miss Shufflebottom looked shocked. She didn't even have a chance to invite the person to come in. The door flew open and Miss Cannington marched into the classroom. I sat down so fast I whacked my bottom on the wooden chair.

At first, our headmistress didn't speak. She just moved her head from side to side. She didn't look happy. In fact, I wasn't sure if the old Cannibal was going to talk to us or eat us. She took a deep breath.

"Agatha, can you come with me, please," she said.

The dirty rascal stood up. She didn't say a word. Instead, she wiped her eyes. Were they tears? Was the most evil girl in the human race crying?

She tucked her chin and followed Miss Cannington out of the classroom. She didn't say anything. She didn't complain. There was no sarcasm, no whining, no giggling, nothing.

It was so obvious now. Everything made sense.

This was turning into the best day ever.

I grabbed Charles' elbow and started shaking. "She's being sent to the headmistress' office," I said.

"She's always being sent to the headmistress' office," he whispered.

Sometimes, he could be dumber than the dumbest dumb person.

"Yes, Detective Dopey, but she's going today. That means she's the thief, Charles. Awful Agatha is the thief!"

CHAPTER TWENTY-TWO

I couldn't remember the last time I'd been so happy. Well, actually, I could. It was when I chatted with my parents on Skype. But I try not to think about Mum and Dad because it's like having a hurricane in my belly. It really hurts.

So I thought about Awful Agatha instead. I pictured all the different, painful punishments she might be suffering in the headmistress' office. They called her the Cannibal for a reason. Maybe Awful Agatha was being stretched out on a rack, like they did in medieval times. Miss Quick-Pants once told me all about the rack. In the olden days, criminals were tied to a rack, which was like a long contraption that pulled their arms and legs until their bones cracked and snapped. I liked the sound of that.

Maybe this school still caned naughty students. Miss Quick-Pants had her cane, which scared all the other royals, but it never bothered me because I was a good girl, most of the time. But a long, bendy cane would whip against Agatha's skin and make it red and sore. The Cannibal seemed like the sort of headmistress who would have a long, bendy cane locked away in her cupboard for emergencies. I don't believe in violence. I'm trained in self-defence. I'm almost a taekwondo expert.

But I'd make an exception for Awful Agatha. She made my

life a misery. She was horrid for no reason. She hated me from the first moment she clapped eyes on me. I knew she'd promised to leave me alone, but that wasn't the real Agatha, the awful Agatha. She would never leave me alone, not until she'd had her revenge for sliding into the pigswill.

But now she couldn't. She was gone. She was outta here. See you later, Awful Agatha. So long. Farewell. Auf Wiedersehen. Good riddance. Get lost.

I had a week of peace coming, a week of peace at least. The little minx should've been suspended for smacking me in the face with a water balloon. And Charles said she'd been a total diva all year long. This was her last straw. She couldn't steal from other students. In fact, I didn't think a week was long enough. She deserved to be suspended for at least a month. A month seemed about right for a disgrace to the human race.

I was just about to lean over and ask Charles if he agreed when the classroom door flew open. Awful Agatha came in first. She looked like she'd been to a funeral. She walked really slowly and kept her head down. The rat-faced troll obviously didn't want any of us to see her weeping eyes.

Miss Cannington followed and closed the classroom door. She looked straight at Miss Shufflebottom.

"Is everything ok?" Miss Shufflebottom asked.

"I'm afraid not," Miss Cannington replied. "I have had a long and difficult conversation with Agatha."

I bet they did. Awful Agatha still wouldn't look any of us in the eye. She was totally guilty and ashamed.

"Could you all stand up please?" Miss Cannington said.

We all looked at each other. Even Miss Shufflebottom seemed confused.

"Stand up, please, children," the Cannibal said again, much firmer this time.

We shuffled to our feet. It didn't make any sense, but nothing about this place made much sense. I looked at Charles. He just shrugged his shoulders. He didn't have a clue either, but then he never does.

"It's not easy for me to say this, but I now suspect that the thief is in this room," Miss Cannington said in her serious headmistress voice.

Finally, we were getting somewhere. Bring on a week with no Awful Agatha! Bring on a month with no Awful Agatha! Maybe she'll get expelled. Bring on the rest of my life with no Awful Agatha! It's party time!

"Could you all pick up your school bags and empty them onto the tables, please."

Now the old Cannibal was making no sense at all. We dumped the contents of our school bags onto our desks. There were reading books, pencil cases and lunch boxes all over the place.

"Come with me please, Agatha," Miss Cannington said.

The pair of them wandered around the classroom, poking their noses into our private stuff on the desks. What cheek!

"Agatha didn't want to come forward. She said she didn't want to tell tales on her friends," Miss Cannington continued.

She was talking gibberish. Awful Agatha didn't have any friends. She just had her laughing hyenas doing whatever she told them to do. She didn't have any real friends, like what Charles and I were.

"But her purse went missing after the assembly and she insists that it went missing in this classroom."

"Miss Cannington, are you sure about this?"

Miss Shufflebottom obviously didn't believe this fairy story either. Even Miss Cannington wasn't sure. She raised an eyebrow at Miss Shufflebottom that told me everything that I didn't want to know.

And suddenly, I knew everything.

I knew what was coming next.

"I have to give Agatha the benefit of the doubt, Miss Shufflebottom. If she says her purse has been stolen, then we must help her try to find it."

In that moment, I hated Awful Agatha.

I hated Awful Agatha more than macaroni and cheese, and not just any macaroni and cheese either, but the powdery one that's made in the packet.

She walked towards my desk with the two teachers.

I hated Awful Agatha more than the doggy poop that the Palace puppies used to leave behind on the kitchen floor.

The three of them stopped at my desk.

I hated Awful Agatha more than the fact that I couldn't go home to my Mum and Dad.

Miss Cannington shook my empty lunch box. It rattled. My empty lunchbox wasn't empty—and I knew why.

The headmistress opened the lunchbox and sighed. "Oh, Sabrina," she whispered.

She took out something that I'd never seen before in my life.

"That's my green purse!" Agatha shouted dramatically.

Of course it was.

The vicious witch finally had her revenge.

CHAPTER TWENTY-THREE

Now the funny thing about Uncle Ernie is he's really handsome. Well, he's not handsome to me, obviously. That would be gross. He's not handsome. He's not ugly. He's Uncle Ernie. That's it. But he's got neat grey hair and a fancy way of speaking that makes women go a bit silly.

At the Palace, the housemaids and cooks always giggled whenever he complimented them. Sometimes, they giggled when he just *smiled* at them. I thought they were all loonies. Maybe it's because I'm a very mature girl for my age. I might even be more mature than the adults. Grown-up women are the ones who go all giggly whenever Uncle Ernie speaks to them. They act like little kids in front of Uncle Ernie. I just didn't get it so, one day, I asked Mum about it.

"Oh, you'll understand when you're older," she said, grinning away as she brushed my hair.

"I want to understand it now," I replied.

"Ok, well, Uncle Ernie is what my mother would've called 'dashing'."

"I know that. He's always dashing about. He runs about like he's got ants in his pants."

Mum laughed. We always laughed together, but I'd rather not think about that now.

"No, this kind of dashing means handsome," she continued.

"Why didn't you just say handsome then?"

"Well, dashing is more than handsome, I would say. Dashing can be handsome and charming and witty and clever, too."

"Well, who else is dashing then?" I wondered.

"Let me think. Ah, yes, do you know the actor George Clooney?"

"No."

"Well, he's dashing, too. Some women think of him in the way that some of the women in the Palace think of Uncle Ernie."

"So these women are all mad as well, then?"

I wasn't buying any of that nonsense. Women lose their minds when they get older. Even if Uncle Ernie was handsome—and he wasn't and never will be—he certainly wasn't charming or witty during our taekwondo lessons.

"I don't think Uncle Ernie is any of those things you said," I insisted.

"No, no," my mother replied. "In a certain light, he looks like Brad Pitt."

I thought he looked more like a gravel pit.

But as I sat in the headmistress' office, I didn't care. In there, Uncle Ernie was doing that thing he does with women, the "dashing" stuff that Mum talked about. And the silly old Cannibal was falling for it!

I still didn't see what was so funny about the tripe coming out of his mouth, but Miss Cannington seemed to be enjoying it and that's all that mattered. Every time Uncle Ernie spoke, she blushed. And then she giggled like a baby. And then she forgot about me for a minute. So I was happy for Uncle Ernie to do his *dashing* magic tricks, whatever they were.

"I'm so sorry to call you in at such short notice, Mr Parslowe," Miss Cannington said.

"Ernie. Please call me Ernie. All my friends call me Ernie."

"Sorry, *Ernie.*"

She said his name funny. Her voice wobbled. Then her cheeks went red. Then she giggled. Then he giggled at her giggling. Then she went even redder, turning into a big, bright traffic light. He smiled at her. She smiled back. And then they giggled again like a couple of kids.

I was the only one in the office behaving like a grown-up.

"Oh, Ernie," she said.

"Oh, Miss Cannington," he replied.

Oh, for heaven's sake, I thought.

"It seems ever so funny calling you Ernie," Miss Cannington gushed.

No, it didn't. She was just being weird again.

"Now where was I?" she asked.

"You were talking about the thefts in the school," Uncle Ernie said.

"Ah yes, it's very unfortunate, Mr Parslowe ... I mean, Ernie. I've been headmistress at this school for twelve years and we've never had so many incidents of stealing in such a short space of time."

Uncle Ernie leaned forward. "That can't be right."

"I'm afraid it is."

"No, it can't be possible that you've been headmistress for

twelve years. You look too young. I thought you'd only just started in the job."

I thought I was going to be sick.

"Ooh, Ernie, you do know how to flatter a woman, don't you?"

Her voice was all high-pitched and fluttery.

"Nonsense. I was just saying to Sabrina the other day that Miss Cannington looked too young to be the school headmistress, wasn't I?"

Uncle Ernie tapped my foot beneath the Cannibal's desk.

"What? Oh yes, that's what he was saying, Miss Cannington, exactly that."

Uncle Ernie wasn't the world champion of little white lies. He was the master of the universe when it came to telling big, fat whoppers.

"Ooh, Ernie, you are far too kind. You're lucky to have such a kind uncle, Sabrina."

I didn't feel particularly lucky. I felt like running from the room, hunting down Awful Agatha and closing her lying gob for good with one of my superb roundhouse kicks. But I just nodded instead.

"That's why this accusation seems so hard to take in."

She pointed at the green purse on the desk. We all looked at Awful Agatha's trap. The purse was old and falling apart. The fake, green leather had mostly peeled off. Why would I possibly want to steal it?

"Miss Cannington, I know Sabrina has had a tough time settling into her new school, but I can assure you that she is not a thief," Uncle Ernie said, finally talking about me, rather than the Cannibal.

"I'm sure she isn't," the headmistress said. "But I cannot be seen to give preferential treatment to any particular student, just as I must take the accusations of every student seriously. Agatha can be ..."

She looked at me, as if she wanted me to finish the sentence. I'd fill in the blanks all right. Awful Agatha is one big blank.

"*Lively*. Agatha can be lively, shall we say, but I have to listen to her nonetheless. More importantly, I have to address the obvious tension between Agatha and Sabrina. That's the deeper issue here."

"I couldn't agree more. That's why I'm here. Could I get a glass of water please, Miss Cannington?"

Uncle Ernie pointed at a jug and some glasses on a cabinet over the headmistress' shoulder.

"But of course."

The moment Miss Cannington turned her back Uncle Ernie whipped his phone from his pocket. He held it over the green purse and pushed a button. A red laser scanned the purse. He winked at me.

"Fingerprints," he whispered, grinning at me.

"What? You can't ..."

Miss Cannington finished pouring water into a glass and started to turn round. "Would you like a glass of water, Sabrina?"

"YES, PLEASE!" I squeaked. "I'm really thirsty, Miss Cannington!"

She turned away again and reached for the jug. Uncle

Ernie continued to scan the purse for fingerprints. He was humming! He was actually humming while committing a crime in my headmistress' office. He had never looked happier.

"Stop it," I hissed.

"Almost done."

I watched the Cannibal pour water into a second glass. I watched Uncle Ernie do something illegal. I waited for us to be arrested. He was smiling. I was sweating. Miss Cannington was turning. Miss Cannington was turning!

I kicked Uncle Ernie under the table. His phone beeped.

"Done," he said, looking really pleased with himself.

Miss Cannington turned round and spotted the phone in Uncle Ernie's hand, near the purse.

"Oh dear, you've caught me red-handed," he said.

"I have," she said.

I felt my bladder bursting.

"I forgot to turn my phone off before the meeting," Uncle Ernie said.

"You did. It's one of our school rules for parents, I'm afraid."

"Sorry, Miss Cannington, it was an urgent business matter."

"Not to worry, Ernie. You're still new here."

"That's true. I'll have to come back so you can show me the ropes."

The blushing Cannibal passed Uncle Ernie his glass of water. Their fingers touched. They chuckled again. My water was dumped on the desk. I had been forgotten about, as usual. But I hadn't forgotten about Uncle Ernie's antics.

He was going to get it when we got home.

CHAPTER TWENTY-FOUR

Uncle Ernie was seriously driving me crazy. He was behaving like a big kid. He whistled all the way home in the van. He always whistled when he was enjoying himself. And then he disappeared into his office full of computers and cables. I moaned about his ridiculous fingerprinting thingy in the Cannibal's office, but he just ignored me.

So I sat in the living room, sulking for a bit. But there's not much point in sulking if no one else can actually see you sulking. So I got up to sulk where he could see me. But he suddenly barged into the living room.

"I've got it," he cried.

He stood in the middle of the room, waving his phone in the air. "I have returned from the dining room with peace for our time."

He was talking gibberish again.

"What are you going on about, Uncle Ernie?"

He shoved his phone in my face. There was a 3D image of that rubbish green purse on the screen. "I scanned the entire side of that girl's purse."

"Awful Agatha. Her name is Awful Agatha."

Uncle Ernie grinned at me. "Is that her full name?"

I crossed my arms in a huff. "No, her full name is Awful Agatha, the most witchy of witches in a disgusting, slime-filled swamp of greasy, toady—"

"Yes, yes, I get it," Uncle Ernie interrupted. "You two don't get on. Well, the good news is I can confirm that your fingerprints were not on that purse."

"I knew that."

"Yes, there were fingerprints belonging to Agatha, Miss Shufflebottom and the endearing Miss Cannington, but none belonging to you."

"How do you know what their fingerprints look like?"

"Oh, that was easy," Uncle Ernie said, leaning over to show me his phone.

"I just used this hacking device to hack into their personal details on a private database called—"

I stuck my fingers into my ears. "Lalalalalala ... lah! I'm not listening! I'm not listening. I don't want to know!"

"Ok, fine, but I have conclusive proof that you never touched that purse."

Uncle Ernie sat back on the sofa, waiting for me to give him a round of applause or something.

"That's brilliant, Uncle Ernie. You're a genius."

"Yes, I think so too."

"*Duh*! I was being sarcastic."

"Oh, were you? It's hard to tell with kids these days."

"And what are we supposed to do with this evidence? Tell the teachers? 'Oh, good morning, Miss Cannington. I didn't steal Agatha's purse because my uncle used an illegal app on his phone to scan for fingerprints.' And he also knows all about your fingerprints because he stole them too.' That's brilliant, Uncle Ernie. Epic!"

He shook his head. "Oh Sabrina, you've still got so much to learn. I'm not confirming your innocence. I knew you were innocent. I'm confirming Agatha's guilt. There were no other girls' fingerprints on the purse, just hers. She set you up."

Uncle Ernie's brain seemed to be turning into mashed potato.

"Of course she set me up! I know that!" I shouted. "I knew that as soon as they found her stupid purse in my bag. How does that help me?"

Uncle Ernie leapt to his feet. "Ok, listen. I wasn't always a handyman at the Palace."

"No, really?"

Uncle Ernie's eyes narrowed. "Is that your sarcasm again? Never mind. Anyway, before I was a handyman, I was a hunter. I worked in a rainforest back home. Well, when I say a hunter, I was a hunter of hunters. Your father employed me to look for poachers. Do you know what poachers are?"

"Yeah, of course, they're people who cook eggs."

"No, not poached eggs, I'm talking about the poachers of animals. They take animals from the wild, illegally."

"Like the way you take fingerprints illegally?"

Uncle Ernie pointed at me. "Ah, that one was definitely sarcasm. Anyway, on one expedition, I was on the hunt for a tiger poacher. He had been trapping and stealing tigers for years. No one had ever caught him. But I did. Do you know how I did it?"

"With your fingerprinting phone?"

"No, come on, think. If someone is catching tigers, how do you protect the tigers? What do you do with the tigers?"

"I don't know. You hide them? You take them away?"

Uncle Ernie wagged his finger at me. "No, you do the opposite. You add tigers. You put more tigers in the forest. You tempt the guy into the forest more often. His greed will always be his downfall. And that's what we did. We took some tigers from the Royal Zoo and released them into a confined space in the forest, watching them the whole time. Eventually, the hunter got too greedy. He tried to steal one of our tigers and we caught him."

I was still mad at Uncle Ernie, but he always told interesting stories. "How did you catch him? Did you shoot him? Did you use your taekwondo? Or your super fast hand-to-hand combat?"

"Of course not. I'm a handyman," Uncle Ernie said, winking at me. "But that's what you have to do with this Agatha."

My eyes lit up. Finally, Uncle Ernie was making sense.

"Yes, that's a great idea," I said. "But where would I get a tiger?"

"What?"

"I'll set a tiger on her, right? With his sharp claws, he would tear her head off and— "

"No, no, no," Uncle Ernie interrupted. "You could lure her into a trap by appealing to her greed. Leave money and purses around the school. Follow her every move. Greed always catches a thief in the end."

I wasn't really sure if that was a good idea. As much as Agatha was awful, it didn't feel right setting a trap. That would make me as sneaky as she was. I wasn't a sneaky person. I certainly couldn't be a sneaky princess.

But then, a light blub exploded in my head. Maybe I could turn Uncle Ernie's trap inside out. I mean, think about that tiger thief. He was caught because there were too many tigers. But what would have happened if all the tigers had suddenly disappeared?

I knew my idea wouldn't make much sense to Uncle Ernie, so I didn't bother telling him. But I knew what I had to do to catch Awful Agatha once and for all. I didn't need to throw money all over the school. I just needed the help of someone who was kind, someone who was caring and someone who was a bit of a weedy coward.

I needed my friend Charles.

CHAPTER TWENTY-FIVE

Charles loves a crisis. He worries all the time. He frowns so much that he looks like someone has drawn lines on his forehead. He would be rubbish in a real emergency, but he was perfect for my plan. I couldn't actually tell him my plan because he would panic and mess it up. I had to make my plan sound like it was his plan and convince him that his secret celebrity friend was in danger.

"This thief is a real pain," I muttered to him in the school canteen.

I had already given Charles my leftover macaroni and cheese, which he was gulping down. So he was in a good mood.

"I know. My mother has told me to hide my lunch money in my sock. Look!"

Charles reached down and pulled out some coins from his sweaty sock. He waved them in my face.

"Ah, put them away. They smell like a bad fart," I said, pinching my nose.

"Yeah, I know. I need some new shoes. But we haven't got much money at home at the moment," he said softly.

He kept staring at his shoes. They were falling apart.

"Anyway, the Cannibal thinks it's me."

"She knows it's not really you. Everybody knows it was Agatha playing a trick."

"Whatever. But the suspicion is no good for me, all this attention."

"Because you're a secret YouTube star!"

"Maybe."

Charles' eyes sparkled. He still couldn't believe that an international YouTube superstar wanted to hang out with him. The way he grinned at me made me feel bad. I convinced myself that this particular white lie wasn't my fault. He had come up with the whole YouTube thing. I just hadn't corrected him. But I still felt guilty. Part of me wanted to tell him the truth. Yet the rest of me knew that if my real secret ever came out I'd have to leave the school and the town.

And I'd have to leave Charles.

He was soppy, too small for a boy and liked detective maths puzzles far too much, but I sort of enjoyed hanging out with him. I didn't like the idea of leaving him. I've already left enough people behind.

"So what can we do?" he asked.

"I don't know. But I'm not sure that the school is doing enough to catch the thief," I said.

"What else can they do?"

"I don't know, if there were more checks maybe, or if the teachers could somehow watch us more in the playground, watch our belongings for us. But that's tough. I mean, they don't have X-ray vision, right?"

"They could do bag checks!" Charles exclaimed.

"Wow, that's an awesome idea. Why didn't I think of that?"

He was so easy.

"But who's going to do them? Students can't do them," I said. "They could plant things on each other. Look what happened to me. Students can't do it."

We watched the teachers on lunchtime duty, patrolling the playground.

"Yeah, students definitely can't do it," I said again.

Charles was being even more dim than usual.

"The teachers could search the bags," he said finally. "Every lunchtime, that's when the thief does all the stealing, right?"

"That's what Miss Cannington said," I pointed out. "It would be really good for me if this stealing stopped once and for all because of my ... *secret*."

I winked at Charles. His face turned into a blob of ketchup. He shoved a final spoonful of macaroni and cheese into his mouth.

"I know what to do, Sabrina. Leave this to me."

"You've got cheese sauce on your chin."

"Oh, right, thanks."

Charles wiped away the yellow gloop on his face. "My plan is epic," he declared. "I don't know how I come up with these great ideas."

He took off like a rocket, flying towards the headmistress' office. And the plan really was epic, too. Charles convinced Miss Cannington that the school was in serious trouble. Like an overexcited dwarf, he must have jumped up and down in her office. He begged her to introduce bag checks before and after lunchtimes and play times. He pleaded with Miss Shufflebottom to monitor the students closely at the canteen tables. He told the canteen cooks to watch the other kids in the queue. He even asked the class prefects to spread his mother's advice. By the next day, everyone was stuffing their cash into their socks. The money stank at lunchtime, especially if there was outdoor P.E. in the morning. The coins weren't so bad, but the notes were soggy and smelled like unwashed armpits.

But the stealing stopped. Just like that.

Charles had never looked happier. After a couple days, he started walking around the playground with a clipboard. He had written a checklist and asked random students loads of questions.

Have you had your bag checked today?

Have you hidden your lunch money?

Is the money in your sock?

Have you finished your mac and cheese?

He asked the last one just to eat any leftovers. He had a huge appetite for a little runt. But the younger kids in school answered all his questions and ticked his boxes. Some of the older boys told him to mind his own business when he asked about their socks though. In fact, Liam, who was a year older and really good at football, threatened to punch Charles in the nose if he went anywhere near Liam's socks.

Apart from that, Charles loved his security project. Whenever he passed me in the playground, he'd wave his clipboard in the air. Sometimes, he tapped his nose, too, which was a little embarrassing. But I was glad he was enjoying himself. It kept him busy while I concentrated on phase two of my project. I was looking for anyone who was acting differently. I was looking for the thief.

Uncle Ernie had *added* more tigers to find his thief. But I had *removed* all the tigers to find mine. All right, I had taken away all the purses and wallets. But it was the same idea, right? With nothing to steal, the thief would have to behave in a different way now.

But nothing changed, not at first. Everyone still did the usual, boring stuff. We listened to Miss Shufflebottom talk about history and geography and maths in class. We went to the field for P.E. and watched Charles fall over a lot. And we went to the canteen and bought lunch. Our daily routines continued. Everything and everyone was normal.

Maybe I was wrong.

Maybe Uncle Ernie was right.

Maybe the only way to catch a thief is to set a trap with money everywhere.

And then, something did change. Something small at first.

Awful Agatha started to wander off at lunchtime. I took no notice in the beginning. She always wandered off. She wandered out of class whenever she couldn't understand the work, which was almost every day. She wandered out of P.E. whenever she'd forgotten to bring a clean kit, which was almost every day. And she wandered off whenever it was time for a shower after P.E, shouting that we were all disgusting and she'd shower when she got home.

But she had never wandered off at lunchtime.

She usually took over one of the canteen tables with her rotten pack of laughing hyenas. They loved lunchtimes. They were like wild animals let out of their classroom cages. They were free to abuse smaller boys and girls and throw food at them.

So I didn't pay much attention at first. It was just Agatha being Agatha. But then she kept vanishing at weird times. She was there in class right up until the bell rang, being her usual, nasty self. And then she'd be in the playground, messing up games and kicking the other kids' balls away. But she'd slip away in the canteen and pop up again in class after the bell. And in the afternoons, she'd be even angrier, arguing with everyone, even Miss Shufflebottom.

So after a few days, I went looking for her. I checked the playground, the field, the classrooms and even the girls' toilets. But she really had vanished.

I was about to give up when I heard a strange, whimpering sound, like a kitten calling for its mother.

The sound was coming from the teacher's private toilets. I tiptoed inside and there she was: Awful Agatha was sitting in the corner, all crouched up and clutching her knees.

She looked like she was ... no. She couldn't be, could she? Girls like Awful Agatha didn't do *that*, did they?

She wiped her eyes quickly so I wasn't sure. But I was sure of one thing. Agatha hadn't been stealing because she was awful.

She had been stealing because she was starving.

CHAPTER TWENTY-SIX

I had pictured this moment millions of times. I could be sitting in class, in the canteen or even on the toilet and I always ended up with the same image stuck in my brain. It was the greatest image of all time. It was just me and her and no one else. We were alone in a room. The door was closed. No one could disturb us. No one could see us. No one could see what I was going to do to her. It would be the easiest fight of my life. Princess Sabrina, the taekwondo expert with awesome roundhouse kicks, versus the girl who slides in pigswill. It was no contest, was it?

But I didn't care.

In my imagination, I squashed her head like a chocolate cupcake. I had so many taekwondo moves. The roundhouse kick was my speciality. But my eagle strike could catch her in the mouth when she least expected it. That'd stop her saying cruel things about me.

But it didn't really matter what punch or kick I used, my daydreaming always had the same ending. Awful Agatha was a heap on the floor, a girly-whirly, weepy mess. And I looked down and laughed at the blubbing bully.

But I couldn't do it now.

I just couldn't.

It wasn't even the secret princess thing or the thought of

being caught by the old Cannibal. It was Agatha's face. She didn't look so awful. In fact, she didn't really look like Agatha at all. She looked fragile, like one of those dolls that babies play with.

"What do you want? Get lost," she said.

She also swore at me. It was Awful Agatha language. But her swearing didn't make her sound awful this time. She sounded a bit pathetic.

"No, I'm not going to get lost," I said, really slowly, because I was still nervous.

"Then you're even more stupid than you look."

"Yeah, I probably am."

"Yeah, you are."

We didn't know what else to say so we stopped talking for a while.

"So you're not going then?" she finally said, sniffing quietly.

She wiped her eyes really quickly. We both knew that I'd seen her wipe her eyes, but we both pretended that I hadn't.

It was weird.

"No, I'm going to stay, if that's all right?"

"Free country," she grumbled.

"Are you sure?"

"Do what you want. I don't care."

I took a few steps towards her. "Thanks. I'll stay for a while."

"Why aren't you playing with your midget?"

"My midget?"

"Charlie."

"You mean Charles?"

"Yeah, the midget."

"He's not a midget."

"He looks like a midget."

"He's just a bit short. And anyway, midget is not a nice word."

"Whatever. He's still a shorty. Why aren't you with him?"

"He's outside, checking everyone's got their lunch money."

"Idiot."

I started to sit down beside Agatha. She looked terrified. "What do you think you're doing?"

"Sitting next to you."

"No one sits next to me. I decide when I want people to sit next to me, right?"

"Yeah, all right. I'll sit here. Is that all right?"

I pointed at the tiled wall, a little further away from Agatha. She checked the distance between us. "Yeah, but no closer," she said.

I took a deep breath. I knew what I was going to say. But I didn't particularly want to say it.

"Are you ..." I began feebly.

"Am I what?" Agatha snapped. Her eyes were like two brown drills digging through my head.

"Are you hungry?"

"What sort of stupid question is that?" she shouted, but her voice wasn't intimidating this time. So I tried again.

"Are you hungry? Have you had lunch?"

"Of course I have, moron. No wonder you hang out with a

midget. You and him should be in the circus. The midget and the moron."

Her insults didn't bother me anymore. They weren't working; they were just words. They used to feel like bullets that went straight through my heart. But now, they were like those soft, foam bullets in toy guns that bounced right off me.

"I watched you at lunchtime," I said, getting more confident. "You didn't line up with the rest of us in the canteen. You didn't buy any food. You didn't bring a packed lunch either. You just disappeared."

"Are you spying on me? You need to get a life. You shouldn't be following me around the school, you know. I could tell the Cannibal."

Her voice was getting louder and higher so I tried to stay calm.

"So you haven't eaten, then?" I said quietly.

"No, I haven't. I've got a stomachache. That's why I'm in here. Satisfied now? ... Good! ... Shut your gob and get out."

Agatha pointed at the door and then shoved her head between her legs.

"Agatha?"

"I said get out."

She refused to look at me. I stood up and thought about leaving. I was trying to help, but she wasn't interested. What else could I do?

"But you didn't eat yesterday, either," I said finally.

Agatha looked up at me. Her eyes were red and scary. "What?" she growled.

"You, er, didn't eat yesterday, or the day before. I watched you. I've been watching you all week."

Agatha started to move. She was suddenly jittery and fidgety. "So you were spying on me?"

"No. I was worried about you. You haven't eaten all week."

"I told you. I wasn't hungry!" she shouted. She swore, too. In fact, almost everything she said had a swear word in there somewhere. The teachers' toilets had never heard so much bad language.

Now she was rocking from side to side. Her body movements were strange. It was scary, in a different way. She didn't seem to be in control of herself.

"But you used to eat more than anybody else in the class. You'd steal leftovers from the rest of us," I said.

"So what?"

"But you stopped eating when the stealing stopped," I continued.

Suddenly, Agatha was on her feet.

"Are you calling me a thief?"

"No, no, I'm not."

"Yes, you are. You're calling me a thief!"

She was hysterical now. In fact, she was screaming almost as much as she was swearing.

"I don't think you're a thief," I said. "I just think you're hungry."

"SHUT YOUR FACE, YOU DON'T KNOW ANYTHING ABOUT ME."

The next thing I knew, I was flying through the air. Even my taekwondo training didn't see it coming. Agatha had pushed me hard in the chest. I flew backwards and smacked my head against the tiled wall. The whole room was spinning around me. Agatha was a blur as she ran towards the door.

"I hate this place," she cried.

She stopped at the door and unzipped her bag, taking out a geography textbook, the really big and boring one. She threw it at the mirror above the sink, shattering the glass into hundreds of pieces. Without thinking, I threw an arm in front of my face to protect my eyes.

"And I hate you," she shouted back at me, slamming the door behind her.

I had imagined so many different meetings between Agatha and me, but none of them ended up like this. This was a disaster, an epic, Sabrina-made disaster that I had to try and fix.

Agatha had already smashed a mirror inside the teachers' toilets. Outside, she could smash up anything.

CHAPTER TWENTY-SEVEN

I had never run so fast in my life. Or maybe I had. It was hard to tell. Uncle Ernie used to make me run around our taekwondo gym and I was pretty quick. But the gym wasn't spinning then. Everything was spinning now. I found it tough to even get to my feet in the teachers' toilets. Finally I reached the door and heard Agatha's angry voice echoing down the corridor. She was swearing at everybody now and shoving students out of the way.

"Wait, stop, Agatha," I called.

But my voice sounded pretty lame. My head was ringing like an alarm clock. I started running, but the school corridor was fuzzy. Luckily, the playground was bright and sunny and that seemed to wake me up a bit. Plus, I noticed that Agatha was slowing down. She hadn't eaten anything for lunch. She had no energy left.

The other students leapt out of her way, as if she were a venomous snake. No one wanted to get attacked. She headed straight for the school gates, but no one had the guts to stop her. They were all cowards. Even her so-called friends, her pack of laughing hyenas, didn't stand in her way. It was obvious that Agatha was going totally crazy. She was trying to run away from school. But no one cared. In fact, they turned away from her. They were probably delighted to see the back of her. I would have felt the same way before I found her in the teachers' toilets.

But the girl sitting on the wet floor of the teachers' toilets wasn't Awful Agatha. She was lost and lonely. She needed help. We all needed help, but we can't always ask for it because we have to keep all these stupid, stupid secrets.

No one understands that more than me.

That's why I ran even faster across the playground. I noticed Charles dashing towards me, still chewing a mouthful of macaroni and cheese.

"What are you doing?" he asked, as cheese sauce dribbled down his chin.

That boy just cannot eat properly.

"Not now, Charles," I replied breathlessly.

I had to save all my energy for catching Agatha. The last thing I needed was a conversation with Charles.

"Why are you chasing Agatha? Is she the thief?"

I raced past him, ignoring his daft questions.

"Is she the thief? Are you being a detective?" I heard his squeaky voice shout in the distance. "Don't chase her, Sabrina. She's running out of school. It's not home time. If you run out of school during school time, it'll be truancy. You'll get suspended for truancy, Sabrina."

Even in an emergency, Charles didn't know when to shut up. I really wanted to hear that, didn't I? I'd already worked out that one or two busybodies would've spotted Agatha and me going in and out of the teachers' private toilets—which we were not allowed to use in the first place. Then, they'd find the smashed mirror all over the floor. What kind of students smashed the mirror of a teachers' toilet? We'd be suspended, maybe even expelled. Agatha was already on a final warning. Now she had smashed a mirror and was about to play truant.

No matter what happened to me, I had to catch her.

I was certainly getting closer. "Agatha, don't run out of school, please," I panted.

I was so out of breath, I didn't even think she'd hear me. But Agatha turned round. "Leave me alone," she said through gritted teeth.

There were tears running down her face. Her sweaty, wet hair was stuck to her face. She looked terrible.

"No, Agatha, you can't," I called, but my voice ran away from me, faster than my useless legs. They were slowing down. My heart thumped against my ribs. My brain banged against my skull. Everything hurt.

But Agatha looked more tired than me. Her arms flapped around like pieces of string. She wasn't even running in a straight line anymore, but zigzagging like a clumsy crab. I was almost behind her now. I tried to reach out and touch her shoulder, but just missed. We were seconds away from the school gates and a world of misery. My world was already the worst ever. But I knew that once I stepped through the school gates, my world would become even worse than the worst world ever.

I was so close now. I could hear Agatha's breathing. I tried one more time.

"Please, Agatha," I wheezed. "Stop running."

She turned around. Her face was a puddle of mucky sweat and tears. She pulled a strange face that wasn't angry or sad. It was, sort of, empty.

"I can't," she mumbled.

And we burst though the school gates and into the street. But Agatha wasn't looking at the street. She was still looking at me. Without looking where she was going, she didn't see the road, the cars or the bright, red bus that was driving straight towards us. She didn't see the traffic because she was still staring at me. It was almost as if she wanted to focus on me and not think about what was coming. Everything was happening so fast. I opened my mouth to scream, but nothing came out.

Then came a scream—the loudest, scariest scream of my life. It was the terrifying shriek of the bus' brakes as the big, red beast screeched towards us.

With her eyes still fixed on me, she took one more step towards the road and closed her eyes.

Now all I could hear was screaming. The bus brakes, students behind me in the playground, strangers on the street—everyone was screaming.

And then, for some strange reason, Uncle Ernie popped into my head. I thought of his taekwondo lessons and the daft things he always said to me. His favourite poem was written by some old, dead bloke called Kipling. It was called *If*, which must be the most boring name for a poem in history. But Uncle Ernie thought it was an epic poem. Whenever he threw kicks and punches at me, he always repeated the same lines from the poem. I can't remember the lines exactly, but they were something about keeping your head when everyone else was losing theirs. At first, I thought the poem was about chickens, because chickens lose their heads all the time. But Uncle Ernie explained that we are sometimes faced with a crisis when everyone around us panics and we must stay calm to fix the crisis. That's what the poem really meant.

And when I heard all that screaming, I finally realised what Uncle Ernie was going on about. Everyone was panicking. They were all losing their heads. But I must stay focused. I must keep calm and carry on. I am Princess Sabrina of the House of Valence. I am not a chicken. I will not lose my head.

So I took off. I dived towards Agatha. Never mind a chicken, I soared like an eagle. I ignored the screaming and flew towards my old enemy. For a split second, Agatha looked shocked.

"What are you ... ARGH!"

She couldn't say anything else because I'd already knocked the air out of her lungs. I grabbed her around the waist. It was a perfect rugby tackle, even if I do say so myself. We flew sideways across the pavement. I must have been running faster than I thought because we seemed to be in the air for ages. Finally, we landed hard against concrete and rolled towards the canteen dustbins. The cooks had shoved them outside the school gates for the vans to collect later.

But we couldn't stop rolling.

We clattered into one of the dustbins so hard, it started to topple towards us.

"Look out!" I cried.

But it was too late. The dustbin began spilling its rubbish—all the leftover food and drink from the school canteen—towards us.

It was pigswill.

It was horrible, disgusting, foul-smelling pigswill!

And it was pouring all over our hair, our faces, our school blazers, everywhere.

Agatha and I sat up slowly. We couldn't really see each other. We were drenched. We wiped our eyes and just looked at each other. She had custard running down her nose. I had soggy potatoes and gravy coming out of my ears.

We couldn't think of anything to say, anything at all.

So we burst out laughing instead.

CHAPTER TWENTY-EIGHT

We had to wait outside the Cannibal's office. Miss Shufflebottom had pulled us out of the pigswill and dragged us through the gates and back into school. She looked more upset than we did. I thought she was going to start crying. Her hands were all clammy and wet, probably because the pigswill was dripping onto her clothes, too. She didn't even think to take us to the toilets first. We stank. We looked like the Vomit Sisters, which is a fabulous name for a pair of punk singers.

We looked like punk. But we smelled like puke.

Miss Shufflebottom had made us sit on either side of a dopey, green plant with rubbery leaves. She probably thought she was keeping us apart, as if a plant could stop us from fighting. She took her bottom and shuffled off down the corridor, leaving us alone. I spotted Agatha wiping her eyes.

"Are you crying?" I asked.

"Get stuffed."

"No, you're not crying."

Agatha turned and glared at me. "What are you going on about, weirdo?"

"I don't think you're crying. We don't cry, do we? Not at our age. That's what I think anyway."

"I think you're a nutcase."

"Yeah, probably."

"Only a nutcase would dive in front of a bus."

I giggled. Then Agatha giggled. And then we both giggled. Now we were the Giggling Sisters.

"Yeah, that was crazy," I said.

"Yeah. Nutcase."

Agatha tapped her foot against the floor. "Thanks."

"What did you say?"

"You heard."

I had heard, so I'm not really sure why I'd asked such a dumb question. I suppose I was shocked, or I wanted to hear someone say something kind about me in this lonely place. Someone who wasn't Uncle Ernie.

"What's it like?" Agatha asked.

She was still looking down at her school shoes. They were covered in green, mushy leftovers from the canteen.

"What?"

"Having no parents."

Now I had a sharp, stabbing pain in my throat. I thought I was being strangled. "I do have parents," I croaked in a choked voice.

"I just can't live with them at the moment," I added.

"Same thing."

"No, it isn't."

"Well, whatever it is, you're lucky."

I couldn't believe what I was hearing. I was many, many, MANY things. I was princess of a dangerous country that I couldn't go back to. I was living with an uncle who wasn't really my uncle who said he was a handyman when he wasn't really a handyman. I was thousands of miles away from the greatest parents in the history of greatest parents. I was acting out this big fat lie of a life that I couldn't tell anyone about and I was covered head to toe in pigswill!

But what I certainly, definitely, absolutely was not, was lucky.

"You don't know what you're talking about," I said, really softly, because my voice was wobbling and this was no time for my eyes to start stinging.

Agatha looked at me for the first time. "Do you see your parents every day?"

"No, not at the moment, but I will soon."

"Then you're lucky. I wish I didn't have to see my parents ever again. I wish my parents were dead."

"No, you don't."

"My Mum and Dad ain't like your parents. They're not like any parents. I see the other kids with their parents. They do all that normal family stuff, like going to the park or to the cinema, but we never do any of that."

"Well, we can't really go to the park or the cinema either," I said, truthfully.

"My Mum and Dad hate each other's guts," Agatha continued. "He never comes home. She never goes out. And when they do see each other, they fight. And then they drink. And then they fight and drink. Sometimes, if I come home too early or I upset them, they will ... ah, you don't care. Nobody does."

"My parents sometimes argue, too," I said. "And they drink wine at dinner parties. Do your parents drink wine at dinner parties?"

Agatha laughed, really sarcastically. "Nah, they just have wine parties."

I didn't get the joke, but Agatha seemed to find it hilarious. She couldn't stop laughing. And then she went strange. Her laughing turned into crying so I had no idea if she was happy or sad.

"You're such an idiot, Sabrina. I thought you were clever. You're just as thick as me!"

Agatha had never called me by my actual name before. It made my belly go funny.

"I probably am a bit thick. I don't understand anything anymore," I sighed. "But I know one thing. I miss my parents."

"I *hate* my parents," Agatha said in a low voice.

"You don't hate your parents."

"You don't know my parents."

We didn't say anything else for a while. I stared at the name on the wooden door. *A. E. Cannington.* I wondered what the Cannibal's initials stood for. Accident and Emergency probably. Agatha and I were one accident and emergency after another.

And then I remembered what caused our latest accident and emergency.

"Your parents don't give you any lunch money, do they?" I asked.

Agatha was back to looking down at her dirty, old shoes. "They don't give me anything."

"You know, my Uncle Ernie thinks he's a bit of a chef. He's not. He just watches *Masterchef* on TV, but he does make too many sandwiches for me every day. I could give you one, if you want."

"I don't want charity," Agatha snapped.

"It's not charity. It's a cheese sandwich."

Agatha thought for a moment. "What kind of cheese?"

"Don't know. Cheddar, I think."

"Is that the dodgy one with the disgusting red skin?"

"That's Edam."

"Yeah. That cheese is well dodgy. What's your cheese?"

"Cheddar cheese. It's not the red one."

Agatha nodded to herself. "Yeah, all right, but not in front of the others. Give it to me in the toilets."

"Not the teachers' toilets though," I said quickly.

We both grinned at each other. I was rather pleased with that joke.

"It don't matter anyway," Agatha said darkly. "The Cannibal will suspend me and then I'll be sent home. I'll have to spend a week with *them*."

"I can't even imagine what a week would be like with my parents," I said, thinking about my old, magical life at the Palace.

"I do. She'll spend all day asleep on the sofa and he'll spend all day shouting. And if he's not shouting, then ... I can't do nothing right, not with *him*."

Agatha started weeping. "I don't wanna be suspended," she whispered.

"You won't get suspended," I said cheerily.

"Of course I will, you Muppet. I smashed a mirror and ran out of school."

"Nah, I'll say the mirror was an accident and you were so upset about the mirror that you got scared and panicked. I'll make up a really convincing story for the old Cannibal."

Agatha rolled her eyes. "No one is gonna believe a made-up story from a Goody Two-Shoes like you. You're not a brilliant liar like me."

I smiled at Agatha. She wasn't awful, really, not anymore.

"You've got no idea," I said. "I tell the biggest lies every single day."

MY CONCLUSION ABOUT ME

So that's my story so far. Well, that's my real story so far. I haven't even started on my fake story yet, the one I'm supposed to write for Miss Shufflebottom. I'll write some rubbish in a minute about being a boring girl from a boring school in a boring town. That'll be my homework. It's meant to be the story of my life, but it might as well be a fairy story. It won't take me long. I'm getting quite good at this writing stuff. And I'm getting really good at lying. I wish I wasn't, but I live in the land of make-believe now.

But it's getting a tiny bit better.

Miss Cannington decided not to suspend Agatha in the end. I made up some nonsense about smashing the mirror by mistake after using the wrong toilets because, you know, I'm a new girl and totally stupid. So I ran right out of school because I was terrified and confused. It was an EPIC lie. My biggest lie yet. I was convinced that the Cannibal would know I was lying. My story sounded completely fake. But like I said, I'm getting really good at lying.

The Cannibal sent final warning letters to our families. Uncle Ernie read the letter and then said the same stuff about keeping a low profile, like it was my fault. Agatha's parents didn't even read the letter. They were still sleeping when the postman delivered the letter, so Agatha tore it up and threw it away.

Her parents sleep a lot during the day.

We have very different families.

But Agatha and I have agreed not to hate each other any more, at least for now. I've promised to give her one of Uncle Ernie's sandwiches every day and pretend it's not a big deal. And she's promised to act like she's not bothered about the sandwiches. We have agreed to do our sandwich deals near the teachers' toilets. That's going to be our secret meeting place from now on.

We have also made a promise that we must keep, no matter what.

No talking about our parents.

Ever.

That's our rule.

She wants her parents to disappear. I want mine to turn up and take me back to the Palace. We both know that we can't get what we want. So we'd rather not talk about it. And anyway, our eyes sting whenever we mention them and we're too old to have stinging eyes at school.

Agatha isn't sure if we should be friends yet, but she's already sent me three messages asking about taekwondo. And she's not the only one!

Cheeky Charles has even asked if Uncle Ernie could give him taekwondo lessons. Uncle Ernie said he wasn't teaching a self-defence class for wimpy kids. So I told Charles I might teach him one or two simple moves when he comes round later. I don't think it's a great idea, but it'll stop him going on and on about his detective maths quizzes and puzzles.

Plus, he still thinks I'm a YouTube superstar! One day, I'll have to find a way to solve that puzzle.

At least he's got no idea about my real secret, for now. Being an exiled member of a royal family in a violent country is not the kind of secret a girl can keep forever.

It's funny though. I don't miss being a princess that much. All I did was wave at people from the car window. I just miss the King and Queen. I think about Mum and Dad every day, especially at bedtime. Bedtimes are the worst. But I know I'll see them again. One day. Definitely. I know I will. Who wants to live without their Mum and Dad? Not me.

I'll just have to put up with this crazy place for now. I know it's not perfect. It's nowhere near perfect. The mac and cheese in the canteen still makes me want to throw up and the school blazer still looks like vomit. But at least I've got my mad Uncle Ernie. And I've still got this story, my true story. I was going to delete the whole lot, but I think I'll keep it now. I might even write new stuff, when I'm in the mood. It feels good being honest. Uncle Ernie makes me tell lies all day long. This is my chance to tell the truth, in private, like volume one of an undercover princess or something. That's a seriously rubbish title. I know it is. I'll think of an awesome title later.

But I really must stop now.

Charles is banging on the door. He's ready for his first taekwondo lesson. He wants me to turn him into a lean, mean, fighting machine. That could take me ages and ages.

But I suppose I'm happy to stick around for a bit longer to help my best friend.

N. J. Humphreys is a bestselling author with 19 titles to his name. An engaging, witty storyteller popular with kids, he grew up in London and saw his first work published at 11, when he was picked to read his funny school journal to the world's toughest audience – hundreds of kids from his council estate. They laughed. He hasn't looked back since.

Among his many children's books, Humphreys' *Abbie Rose and the Magic Suitcase* series are entertaining eco-adventures about a smart, feisty girl on a mission to save endangered animals. He is currently working on the animated TV series with an international broadcaster.

He is based in Singapore.